Doorway
Through The Oak

By Philippa Drakeford

To my family, with gladness for my childhood.
And to the hollow oak.

With thanks to Pat Mead for her help.

A Quirky Dragon Book
from Appleseed Press
Beyond the ordinary
- stories for young people by Philippa Drakeford

quirkydragon@yahoo.co.uk
www.appleseed-press.co.uk

First published in Great Britain 2009
by Appleseed Press, Essex, England
Printed by Cpod

A catalogue record for this book is available from the British Library.

ISBN 978-0-9548572-8-8

Printed and bound in Great Britain
by Cpod, a division of The Cromwell Press Group, Trowbridge

CHAPTER ONE

"Rowan?"

Rowan trudged along, head down, hands thrust into her coat pockets, mouth tightly closed and eyes screwed up against the horrible weather. The icy wind was flinging stinging sleet into her face. Her little sister Rosie was walking in front of her, stomping solidly along, her woolly hat pulled well down over her ears.

"Rowan?"

"Huh?"

Rosie half turned. "Don't you wish?"

"Wish what?"

"I *said,*" Rosie looked impatient. "Don't you wish it'd snow?"

"Suppose," said Rowan.

"You said you did this morning."

"I know."

"Mum and Dad say it used to snow when they were kids. It never does now."

"It did a couple of years ago. Three years."

"I don't remember."

"You were only three. I was seven, I remember."

Rosie scrunched up her face. "I *think* I remember... it was before I went to school. *Yonks* ago. It didn't stick for long. I wish it'd stick. And we could make snowballs and slide on a sledge like Mum and Dad used to."

"Global warming," said Rowan.

"Not fair, the grown ups polluting everything so we can't get snow. S'not proper freezing, not enough for snow, only this nasty old sleet! I hate sleet, I wish..." Rosie grumbled on.

If only, thought Rowan, snow was all I had to worry about! Rosie was lucky, she was happy enough in school. Okay, sometimes she fell out with her friends, but they made it up again soon enough. She wasn't being –

Rowan didn't want to think about it. It sounded pathetic, it sounded wet. I mean, who was Maxine anyway? Why did what she say matter?

But it did.

She squinted at the sky, grey with heavy cloud. The road under her feet was grey, with brownish mud and puddles of wet, freezing water. Rosie was right - snow would be nice, a blanket of white to cover all this dullness. The hedges were bare, with prickly twigs, the grass dull green, or faded beige from the tall dried out stalks which had been so tall and lush in summer. Now it was winter, long past the joy of Christmas and New Year, Rowan was back at school, and spring seemed a million miles away. So did home, although it was only ten minutes walk from the bus stop to there. It was a country road without a pavement, and the girls knew to keep well into the side, away from the cars. Occasionally one would swish past.

"Here we are!" Rosie called out, and broke into a run. "Bet Dad's made us some hot chocolate!"

Rowan followed her sister through the wooden gate, up the drive and turn left, into the front door of the whitewashed stone house, which was called Oakland Farm. It wasn't a proper farm any more, the only animals they kept there were chickens and the guinea pigs. There was a vegetable patch out the back, though.

Rosie was burbling about the guinea pigs now as she pulled off her coat and hung it up, followed by her hat. "D'you think Mohican and Pickle are cold? I put them in a big bundle of hay this morning. You reckon they've eaten it already?"

"Hello there." It was their Dad, Bob Meadows. He gave first Rosie then Rowan a hug. "Mum'll be back soon, she's just getting in the provisions." It was a phrase he always used to mean she'd been doing the shopping. "How was school?"

"Hiya, Dad, fine - can we have hot chocolate?"

"It's in the saucepan now, just waiting."

"Goody!"

"And how was school for you, Rowan?"

"Fine," lied Rowan, not wanting to admit that she was being –

It was good to be out of the icy wind, though. They both went into the warm kitchen, where Bob Meadows poured the hot chocolate into mugs.

"I'll just check on 'em," said Rosie, going through the wooden door on the left of the oven and into the utility room, which had shelves full of boxes and jars, a huge chest freezer and the washing machine in it.

Mohican and Pickle normally lived in a hutch outside, but had been brought into the utility room to keep them warmer in the winter. When you switched the washing machine on, which was right next to their hutch, they squeaked madly and rushed around in a panic for the first few minutes, before getting used to it. They were both a mixture of ginger, black and white, and their fur stuck out in all directions. Rowan had named Mohican for the fur that stuck straight up between her ears, just like a Mohican haircut. Rosie opened the hutch and picked up both guinea pigs. They chirped at her, and she crooned back.

Rowan settled next to Rosie on the sofa, mug of hot chocolate in one hand, Mohican warm and furry on her lap. She stroked Mohican and she whuppled, which is what the girls called the guinea pigs' happy sound. Pickle whuppled too, and Rosie mimicked her, making the noise people make when they're imitating a machine-gun - a-a-a-a-a, only less harshly and with her mouth closed.

Rowan smiled a bit, glad she was able to make her pet happy. Her body relaxed and she sighed with relief.

School was over for another day. She was home safe,

there would be supper, and homework, and a bedtime story. Now she could forget, for a few precious hours, that she was being bullied.

Chapter Two

That Sunday was chilly, but the sun actually shone, pale yellow white, from behind straggly clouds. They both put on old jeans, coats, and Wellington boots to go outside. The vegetable patch looked bare, except for a few remaining winter cabbages, and most of the plants in the herb garden had lost their leaves for winter. The blackberry hedge was bare, too, with spiky twigs. Rowan remembered last autumn when it had been loaded down with ripe, juicy blackberries. They had picked until their fingers were purple from the juice - and their tongues too, as they had had to sample some, of course. "Quality control," their Mum, Jenny, had said with a smile, popping one into her mouth. They had all laughed. That had been fun, and then they'd had the delicious blackberry and apple crumble for Sunday pudding…

Rowan's smile faded. That was over now.

On the other side of the blackberry hedge was a field which belonged to the Robinsons, who were farmers. You could reach it through a gap in the far left hand corner of the hedge, and just a few paces from that gap was an old oak tree.

"Let's go and climb the tree," suggested Rosie.

"Okay," agreed Rowan. They were both very fond of the oak tree. They liked to climb it, especially in summer, when the green leaves made a thick canopy. Sitting up there was a perfect place to let their imaginations run free, play games, tell stories, and eat their Saturday sweets.

The branches and twigs were totally bare now, of course. There would be acorns in the autumn, each held in a perfect little cup. The kind of cups that fairies might drink nectar out of, Rosie had said. Or dormice might, they could hold it in their little paws. Dormice didn't do that, Rowan had said, which had caused a brief quarrel.

They strode over the clumps of ragged grass, avoiding the thistles and stinging nettles, until they reached the tree. There was bare earth around it, hard and smooth from many footprints. Rowan put a hand out and touched the bark, which was rough with deep grooves in it. It was soothing to touch.

"Tell you what," began Rosie, who had crouched down on the ground.

"What? What're you doing down there?"

"There was a beetle. Tell you what, there's a sort of gap between the roots."

"Is there? I've never noticed that before." Rowan bent down. "Suppose it's usually got tall plants most of the year, covering it up."

"Yeah. Tell you what, I reckon I could crawl inside it."

"You'll get dirty," warned Rowan, not that she particularly minded, but, as the older sister, she felt responsible for Rosie.

"We're in old clothes," justified Rosie, lying down flat on her tummy. "And anyway, it's not muddy. The ground's quite hard, see." She patted it with the flat of her hand.

"Okay then, go for it." Rowan looked on with interest as her little sister wriggled forward like a caterpillar. She ducked her head and it disappeared into the gap, followed by her shoulders, then her tummy. There were just two boots now, waggling around on the end of her legs.

"What's it like?" called Rowan.

"Cool!" Rosie's voice came back muffled, but excited. "There *is* a hollow. Big enough for one! And there's this sort of shelf thing… and there's a couple of acorn cups… a woodlouse… two woodlice. Oh, and there's the beetle!"

"Can I see?"

"Hang on." There was a pause, then Rosie squirmed out backwards, her cheeks pink and dark eyes bright with excitement. "Go on! I think it's big enough. It's lovely, like a little home for Mrs Tiggywinkle or something! Or squirrels, or little gnomes."

Rowan lay down, the ground hard under her body, and pulled herself forward on her elbows. She had to wriggle a bit to get her shoulders through, but she managed, and then then the top half of her was inside the hollow tree. It was difficult to see upwards, but by rolling her eyes up, she could just see a spiky jagged ceiling of rotten wood. The walls were quite smooth, and so was the smooth earth floor. It was like a miniature Peter Pan's den, she thought. She'd always liked the idea of that, an underground den. She picked up an old acorn cup, and placed it over her thumb, then to her left she saw that the wood had formed a kind of shelf, as Rosie had said. It was about the size of her hand, with a smooth curved underside, and a rougher curved top, rather like a bowl. She felt it - so smooth, astonishingly smooth and shiny. She put the acorn cup on it.

"Come on, you've been ages!" complained Rosie impatiently.

"Okay." Rowan wriggled out backwards, panting a bit, and stood up.

Rosie hopped about with excitement. "D'you think we could make it our den?"

"Well, there's only room for one at a time… it would be good, though. A den in a hollow tree. Like Sam in *My Side Of The Mountain.*"

"What's that?"

"One of Dad's favourite books. It's about this American boy who goes and lives in the woods for a year. He lives in a hollow tree and gathers all his own food, and he has a falcon called Frightful. Dad says he used to dream of living in a tree when he was a boy in London. I s'pect he'd read it to you if you ask."

They spent a couple of hours at the oak tree, then it clouded over and began to sleet. Rowan liked Sundays because it meant Sunday dinner - roast beef and Yorkshire pudding, in this case, and Sunday pudding, which was plum crumble made with frozen plums from last summer.

The only problem with Sundays was it was too near Monday. School loomed. And Maxine.

"I think five goes in that square."

"Yes. Because that leaves a space for six."

Rowan was in the playground with Sarah and Becky, who were bent over a Sudoku book. Both of them enjoyed Maths and Science, and they were more friends with each other than they were with Rowan. Sarah was quite slender with blue eyes and straight blonde hair. Becky was a stocky, round-faced girl with wavy mouse-brown hair and brown eyes. They weren't unkind to Rowan, but she found it difficult to join in their conversations, because she wasn't into Maths or Science like they were. She had never been round to either of their houses.

"Ooh look! The ginger, the spastic and tin grin metal mouth! Well, I wouldn't recommend *you* for a modelling agency!"

Rowan jumped. It was Maxine, blonde hair impeccable, head tilted arrogantly, one hand on her hip, surrounded by her gang of girls.

Becky closed her mouth, so her brace couldn't be seen. Sarah rolled her eyes.

"Oh, look, the baby's dribbling! Is it time to change her nappy yet?"

"Sarah's not a baby!" Rowan defended her. To her shame,

her voice wobbled.

Maxine retorted by sticking her tongue in between her teeth and lower lip, and making grunting noises to imitate Sarah. Her gang all snickered, as though it was the best joke in the world.

Sarah had cerebral palsy, which meant she couldn't speak clearly, and sometimes her head would nod or her arms and legs twitch without her being able to control them. She was in an electric wheelchair, which she directed with her right hand, and there was a built in communicator to 'speak' for her.

Sarah's communicator spoke now: "I bet you do not know what the square root of 289 is." Maxine never quite knew how to respond to this kind of thing. Her lips tightened, and she brushed a strand of her long, blonde hair away from her face.

After a suitable pause, Sarah replied: "It is seventeen. Can you tell me what fifty-two times forty-seven is?"

Maxine wasn't standing for that. She and her gang stalked away.

Becky shrugged, caught Sarah's eye. "I think eight goes in this square," said Sarah, and they returned to their Sudoku. But Maxine cornered Rowan later when she was on the way to the toilets. "Ginger. You're a freak. No wonder you hang out with that spastic!"

Anger choked Rowan, she clenched her fists, and gulped. "D-don't call her that!"

"Why not? It's what she is." Maxine smirked. It was much more satisfying to say horrible things about Sarah to Rowan, because Rowan would get angry and upset. Her little gang snickered, their eyes gleaming.

Rowan went stiff with rage. She wanted to smash Maxine's grinning smug face in, her perfect nose and mouth and pretty blue eyes, eyes that would look so innocently at grown ups, eyes that made them think Maxine was a sweet little girl.

In reality, Maxine specialised in devastating you with a look and a few words. Those pretty blue eyes would flick up and down, condemning you instantly.

"Do you really think your coat's fashionable, Rowan?" she asked in a sugar-spiteful voice, as Rowan blundered past them and pushed the door of the Girls Toilets open.

"Like, hello?" Maxine called after her. "Where'd you *get* that, a jumble sale?"

Rowan barged into the toilet cubicle and sat down, with the tinkling giggles of Maxine and her gang ringing in her ears. She put her head in her hands.

In Rowan's case it was true that some of her clothes came from jumble sales. Mum and Dad spent so much on the mortgage that they had to save money somehow, so they didn't do things like going abroad on holidays, or buying lots of expensive toys and clothes for Rowan and Rosie.

"If you have fewer treats, you appreciate them more when you do have them," Mum had told them one day when they were complaining that everybody else had more things than them.

But Maxine wouldn't understand that. Looking fashionable was everything, you had to have the right clothes, the right hair, the right body, the right look. And if you didn't, look out.

She is cool, thought Rowan, she is popular, and everybody wants to be in her gang. All the girls, anyway.

I'm pathetic, Rowan told herself. Why can't I be confident like Sarah?

Sarah wasn't officially one of the 'cool' ones, but she did have self-confidence. She didn't let the things Maxine said bother her.

Maybe it's easy to pretend you don't care if you have an electronic voice. It doesn't wobble, unlike mine. Why can't I not care? It's only words.

It's me. There's something wrong with me. Why can't I be confident like Sarah?

Or cool like Maxine? Maxine, pretty and popular, with girls competing to be in her gang. Life would be so easy if Rowan was like Maxine.

It was Thursday night and Rowan couldn't sleep. She tried one way, then another, but it was no good. She sat up, and looked around the large, long bedroom that she shared with her sister. Her back was to the wall with the two windows, moonlight shone dimly through the half-open curtains, so she could see all the familiar objects: the two cupboards, a very large and well stocked bookshelf, and a table and chairs, all of them wooden. Then their doll's house, and there was the rocking sheep, which is like a rocking horse, only it's a sheep, with real fluffy sheepskin sides. She used to ride on it when she was little, and pretend to feed it grass and flowers. Once she had brought it out onto the lawn, then forgotten about it and gone in for lunch, only for it to be drenched in a sudden summer shower. She had been mortified, but Mum, a hairdryer and the airing cupboard had solved the problem… that had seemed such a disaster at the time, but she'd give anything for that to be her worst problem now!

Why couldn't she stop thinking about it? One of the chime bars that hung from the ceiling glinted and made a faint tinkling sound. The door was to her right. To her left was Rosie's bed. A streak of silver moonlight shone from the gap between curtain and wall and onto her sister's face, eyes closed, thumb in mouth, her furry toy crab, Sideways, snuggled against her cheek. Oh, to be six years old, to be like Rosie with no problems!

It kept on and kept on going through her head, her mind just wouldn't stop. Maxine's sneering face. The others all staring at her. Her own helplessness. They had got her alone in the playground, walking behind her at first.

"Ginger? Hey, ginger? Gin-ger!" in a sing-song voice. Muffled snickers.

It was better to answer. If you said nothing, Maxine just repeated the question again and again, adding things like, "What's wrong? Why won't you answer? You're not *upset* are you?" with this sickening fake sympathy.

"What?" Rowan turned around to face them, trying to stand tall, to look confident, but cringing inside. They clustered round her with eager faces, like vultures around a carcase.

"That man who came to the school concert at Christmas," began Maxine.

"The man with the ginger woman, your Mum. She's even more ginger than you," added Cressida, who was currently Maxine's second-in-command.

"Is he your father?"

"Yeah," replied Rowan shortly.

Maxine smiled triumphantly. Rowan's stomach sank - she knew she had somehow fallen into a trap, though she didn't know what it was yet.

"He's not your *real* father," said Maxine. "He's white and you're not."

"So? I've got two fathers, so what?" Her voice wobbled. Calm. Don't let it bother you.

"Well, it's *obvious* your real father's black, I mean, because of your skin colour." She made it sound as though her skin was a horrible colour. Rowan had always liked being golden brown. Until now.

"Yes, he's black."

"And he ran off." Maxine had her head on one side, her voice lowered with fake sympathy.

"He didn't run off."

"Oh, yeah. Well, he's not *here,* is he?"

"He visits."

"Oh, yeah?" Maxine gave her a pitying look, as though she was lying. "Tell me something, I've always wondered. I mean, you should know, being half black…"

"What," sighed Rowan, wearily.

"What is it with black men? Why do they always have babies and then run off?"

"They don't. And that's racist."

"No, it's not, I'm just stating a fact. Black men leave their babies, they're always doing it." She sounded so *reasonable,* both her hands palm up.

"No they aren't! Lots of black men are good fathers!" Rowan's voice wobbled again.

"Yeah? Well how come your father left you, then? If it's not because he's black, then it must be because there's something wrong with *you*… I know what it is. It's because you're a ginger. He must've taken one look at you and nearly thrown up!"

She snickered, and so did the others.

"I mean, what a shock! He'd be expecting a black baby like him, and there's this ginger! Wow, you must've been really ugly to make him run off. You must've been totally gross as a baby."

I won't cry, thought Rowan. I will *not* cry. I won't give her the satisfaction. But it felt as though she had swallowed a spiky metal egg, and it was in her throat, hurting her.

The bell had gone, and saved her, but it had been a horrible day.

I'm pathetic, she told herself now. Useless. If I wasn't I could stand up to her. It's just words. It's not like she's beating me up, or stealing my things, or proper bullying like that. It's just *words.*

Words that hurt.

Why do I let her get to me? Pathetic. Useless.

I wish I looked like her, she's pretty and popular. It's all right for her. Nobody picks on her for being out of fashion.

Rowan closed her eyes and thought about her reflection in

the mirror. She had stared at herself when she was getting ready for bed, toothpaste on her brush ready to clean her teeth. She had examined her own face, looking for some clue as to why Maxine had picked her out, why Maxine's words crumpled her up inside.

Rowan's eyes were deep green like her Mum's. Her nose and mouth were a similar shape to her father's. Her hair was chestnut brown, and when sunlight shone on it, it was red as rowan berries, rather like her mother's hair, only Mum's was lighter. It had been curly when she was little, but it had straightened out and now was only slightly wavy. It was thick and lustrous, cut to jaw length.

Part of my hair comes from Daddy Taylor, she told herself. Taylor Rivers's hair was curly rather than frizzy. He said that it was from Taino ancestors. They were the original people on Jamaica, before the Europeans invaded and brought African slaves, and killed most of the Taino. One must have survived long enough to have children with one of the Africans, and some of Daddy's family had had hair like that ever since. You couldn't tell much about his hair, though, because he wore it in little plaits.

Now Rosie was obviously Bob Meadows's daughter, they were both stocky and round-faced with brown eyes, and rosy cheeks. Bob's hair was a darker brown than Rosie's, almost black, but they looked very alike.

Rowan thought about earlier that night, when Dad was in their bedroom. They shared a bedroom, which was fine, it was large, plenty of room for two beds and all their things.

Bob had picked up Rosie's toy crab, which was her

favourite, and looked at it thoughtfully. "Shall I throw Sideways out of the window?" he suggested.

"No, no!" shrieked Rosie, dashing towards him, and trying to grab Sideways out of his hand. Bob held Sideways high out of her reach, while she circled round him, arms stretched high, jumping up and down. "Are you sure? Don't you think he'd enjoy the flight? Perhaps he'd bounce, shall we see?"

"No, no, no! Give him back, Dad, give him back!" squealed Rosie. Both of them were enjoying it, dark brown eyes shining, faces red with laughter. Finally, Bob opened his hand and let Sideways drop, Rosie grabbed hold of her crab, cradled him and crooned: "Don't worry, Sideways! Won't let you go back to mean old Dad!" while glancing sideways at her father, who laughed and ruffled her hair.

They were alike, thought Rowan. She loved Dad, of course, and he loved her, but perhaps it wasn't as good as having your own father living with you… her Daddy Taylor, she loved him too, but he couldn't be *here.*

She thought of him, Daddy Taylor, her father. He phoned regularly, he always remembered her birthday and Christmas, he always had presents and a card for her. On her birthday, every year, he would be there without fail. He had changed the dates of gigs before now. "No, I can't do March the third," he would say, "It's my daughter's birthday. How about the week after?" He was a good father. It was just he and Mum didn't get on well enough to stay together after Baby Rowan was born, and then Mum had met Bob Meadows and they had got married and moved here and had Rosie, and she was glad - she loved Bob as her second

Dad and she loved Rosie as her little sister…

Why did Maxine make her feel there was something wrong about it? Why was she always picking on her?

Was it because Rowan was the only mixed race girl in the school? Almost everybody else was white, was that it?

Rowan thought even if she was white too, that she would somehow still be the odd one out.

Just because of who I am. Just because I don't care about being in fashion, and celebrities, like the others do. Well, I sort of care because they get at me, but I'm not interested in it. It's not interesting, it's rather stupid really. But it would be good if I had the stuff. Maybe then they'd leave me alone.

What is wrong with me? Why am I so pathetic? Why won't she leave me alone? Why can't I think of smart answers, something to shut her up?

Round and round and round in her head.

It was no good. She just couldn't sleep. She got out of bed and padded over to the window, drawing back the curtain. A silver half moon shone in the sky, and there were stars.

All this pressure, she couldn't stand it any more, she would scream!

Perhaps she'd feel better if she went outside.

Rowan didn't know quite why she thought that, but she remembered the soothing oak tree. She wanted to be there, wrapped up in its treeness, curled up like a safe womb, away from all hurt.

It was frosty outside, and her feet crunched on the glittering grass. She had put her boots on, and jumper and jeans over her pyjamas. Her shadow was very long and very black. Everything looked bigger in the dark, the spiky twigs of the blackberry hedge quite alarming, like barbed wire. But she slipped through the gap, and crept over the field towards the gnarled lumpy shape of the oak tree, with its two main branches spread out from the trunk like arms widened from someone's body, some giant tree-creature, beckoning her closer.

Rosie sat up in bed. She had heard Rowan get out of bed, and had sleepily assumed she was just going to head for the loo, and then come back. But instead there were cautious swishing sounds, and little clumps - Rowan getting dressed. And then quiet footsteps out of the room. Where was she going? Was she going to creep downstairs and have a midnight feast or something?

If so, then Rosie didn't want to be left out. Hastily, she slipped out of bed, pulled on a jumper and jeans, and pattered downstairs after Rowan. Who was, strangely, going out of the front door. Why was she doing that? Puzzled, Rosie grabbed her purple woolly hat, jammed it on her head, stepped into Wellington boots, and followed. An owl hooted, making her jump. She could see a line of footprints, dark in the white frosted grass. She crept after them.

She was just in time to see her sister's legs and feet disappear into the hollow oak. Which was weird, because Rowan hadn't been able to fit her whole body inside last time.

And there was *light* shining from the hole in the tree, blue-white light.

What was that? Aliens? Fairies?

Alive with excitement, Rosie got down and crawled through the tree after her sister.

Chapter Three

The pale gold sunlight shone on sparkling snow, the shadows as blue as the sky. It wasn't night any more, it was day. There was no sign of the normal things, their house, the farm buildings, the field. Instead they were surrounded by bare trees, as far as the eye could see. It was a forest.

At first they were too astonished to speak. They stood up and stared.

"Snow!" exclaimed Rosie in delight.

"What happened?" wondered Rowan.

"We're in another world!" declared Rosie.

"Maybe. Or maybe we've gone back in time." Rowan

looked around cautiously, then back at the oak. There was a way through, she reassured herself, in case they needed it. "To before the Robinsons' farm existed, when it was just a forest here."

"I think it's another world. It's magic!" Rosie stretched out her hands, beaming, then began to take a few steps forward, her feet crunching in the snow. She bent to touch it with her fingers, lifted it up to her face. "Cold! It's real," she confirmed, hastily brushing it off again by rubbing her hand against her jeans.

"Yeah, it is," agreed Rowan. This was real. This wasn't just a dream. She dug the toes of her boots into the snow, shovelling some of it aside, and looked to see old, dead brown leaves underneath. "Oak leaves," she observed.

"Of course, we came through an oak," said Rosie.

"Lots of them are oaks," said Rowan. "I can tell by the twisty shape of the branches and the grooves in the bark. Oak bark is rough."

"What about those ones? The grey ones?" Rosie pointed.

Rowan went over to one, and took a twig in between her fingers. There were black buds on the end of it. "Ash," she identified. She let the twig go and it sprang back, sending a little shower of snow down onto the floor of the forest.

"And those are silver birches," she added, loving the slender trees with their bark as white as the snow.

"I know *them,*" said Rosie. "They're easy!"

"Look how each twig is outlined in snow," marvelled Rowan. "It's beautiful."

"Yeah," agreed Rosie, then something occurred to her.

"D'you think we'll meet a Witch on a sledge and she'll put a spell on us? D'you think this wood's under a spell to make it always winter?"

"Like Narnia? No, I don't think so." Rowan smiled. "I think it's just ordinary winter. Listen." They stood still. The forest was very quiet, but there was just a slight chuckling swishing sound. "A stream. Let's go and see," suggested Rowan.

"Okay," agreed Rosie.

They set off through the snow, which crunched satisfyingly underfoot, and their breath puffed out in steam.

"Hang on!" Rowan stopped, alarmed. "There's loads of oaks - how do we know which is ours?"

"Easy!" Rosie laughed. "We follow our footprints!" She pointed to where their tracks were clearly laid out, blue in the shadows.

"Oh, yeah!" realised Rowan and laughed. She hadn't felt so carefree in ages. She looked up at 'their' oak. There was a garland of pale green mistletoe hanging from one branch, its berries white, like little moons. She raised a hand to salute it, then turned and went on with Rosie by her side.

"Look!" Rosie pointed to a track of little round footprints. "What's that?"

"Don't know. Fox maybe?" suggested Rowan. "I expect most of the animals are hibernating, though."

"Look!" exclaimed Rosie, and pointed ahead and to their left - it was a red deer, running through the trees on delicate legs.

"Wow!" Rowan smiled. "Fantastic!"

The deer paused, bright russet against white snow. The sunlight fell on it, deepening and brightening the beautiful colour, and it shone on red holly berries and dark green spiky holly leaves, making the nearby bush glow like jewels. The deer's ears swung round, then it skipped away, and was gone.

The girls carried on walking, all eyes.

"That's an apple tree," identified Rowan, pointing to the squat gnarled branches and spiky twigs.

"There's the stream," said Rosie.

The stream, which was two or three paces wide, ran down a slope, and through a clearing. They passed a few bare bushes of hazel and hawthorn to reach it, and a couple of alder trees. There were willows growing on either side. There was ice at the edges of it, and pale, dried grasses, but the middle was water, flowing freely.

Rosie bent and dipped a finger in. "Phew! Ice cold!" she exclaimed, and took her rather pink finger out again.

"Clear, though," observed Rowan. "You can see the bottom."

"Can't see yours," chuckled Rosie, "All covered up in jeans and knickers!"

"Very funny!" Rowan swiped at her little sister, who hopped back like a robin, brown eyes bright, scooped up some snow and threw it at her. It burst and scattered on Rowan's sleeve.

Then they were laughing, shrieking, chasing each other in and out of the trees, scooping, pressing and throwing snowballs, breathing the crisp cold air, drinking in the winter sunlight.

At last they slowed, panting, red-faced. They had come to the edge of the forest. There were bushes here, bare spiky hawthorn, bare hazel and dark green holly, which gave way to russet, snow-covered bracken, and then a fairly smooth land, flat for a few yards, then rising to a slope. Here and there, an old pale beige stalk, the remains of summer grasses, stuck out of the top of the snow.

The snow was deeper here, nearly up to Rosie's knees as they plodded forward, their feet making prod-prod noises. There was a dead tree nearby, which had fallen, and lay half-covered with snow. Rosie waded through a drift to the tree, and examined it. "I've got an idea," she said, putting her fingers under the bark and hauling. It was loose, and came off in a shower of small chips of wood.

"What are you doing?" asked Rowan.

"Just a - hmph - minute -" panted Rosie, walking backwards until she had pulled off a piece almost as big as herself. She laid it on the ground so the edges curled up. It was about as thick as Rowan's thumb. "I think," began Rosie, "that we can use this as a sledge."

Rowan frowned. The movement of a robin caught her eye as it darted down to the bare trunk, and began pecking at it, searching for grubs and insects which had been hidden in the bark. "Okay, let's try," said Rowan.

They dragged the bark half way up the slope, then Rosie sat in it, clinging onto the sides, Rowan pushed, it slid a bit, got stuck halfway, then slithered slowly down to the flat ground.

"Nearly," said Rosie. "Come on, you try!"

So they took it in turns, and got quite fast by the end, both panting and breathless. Then the bark cracked under the strain and that was the end of their sledging.

"Never mind," said Rosie. She grinned. "It was cool, wasn't it? Neat idea of mine!"

"Hush!" Rowan put a hand on Rosie's arm, and nodded upwards. There was a hare, as white as the snow, sitting up on its heels to watch them. One long ear twitched forward. Then it turned and ran away, leaping gracefully along the top of the ridge and out of sight.

"It's big for a rabbit," remarked Rosie.

"It's a hare. They are bigger," said Rowan. "Let's climb up and see."

It was a laborious business, making their way up the slope, but neither of them stopped, or turned back.

"What's that?" wondered Rowan.

"What's what?" asked Rosie.

"That sound. Can you hear it?"

Rosie listened intensely. "A sort of… swishing, rushing sound…"

"I know what it is! It's the sea!"

They reached the top of the ridge, and then they saw it, spread out before them, the land sloping down for about a hundred yards then stopping abruptly, and beyond it, the deep turquoise blue of the sea, the waves capped by white foam, breaking against the rocks and the golden sand of the beach. Wind blew the taste of salt onto their lips, and that unmistakeable briny seaweedy smell to their noses.

"Cool!" squealed Rosie, rushing forward.

"Rosie, stop!" Rowan grabbed her by the back of her coat, yanking her backwards. "Don't go dashing off the edge of a cliff! You'll hurt yourself!"

Rosie wriggled out of her grasp. "I won't! I just wanted to see if there's a way down!"

"Well, go slowly!"

"This place is magic, maybe we can fly!" reasoned Rosie.

"And maybe we can't. What would I tell Mum and Dad if I came back without you cos you'd drowned? Or had to drag you back with two broken legs? How would we explain that one?"

"Oh, okay," conceded Rosie.

So they went forward carefully, and discovered there was a long spit of land that jutted forward and became the top of rocks, gradually descending into the sea. The rest of the land had been eaten away by the ever-pounding waves, and went straight from cliff to beach. They walked along the top of the land, which was covered with tough short grass. The wind from the sea had blown most of the snow away.

"It's almost like a pier," said Rosie. "Rocky Pier."

"Yeah, it is. Only no fruit machines or candyfloss," agreed Rowan. "Look at those smooth grey rocks down on the beach there. They're like giant pebbles." She pointed to their right.

"Oh yeah - ooh! One of them moved!"

"Don't be silly - sorry, I mean, rocks don't move!"

"It did, it did!"

"Which one?"

"There!"

"It's still now, it - oh! It did move! Hey, it's not a rock at all, it's a seal!"

"Oh, yeah! It's got a head! Look, they're all seals, all of them!"

"There must be about a dozen!"

"Let's go down and say hello!"

"I dunno, that male looks ever so big. I've seen them on TV, fighting. They bite, do lots of damage."

"But he's so fat," giggled Rosie, "And he's got no legs, none of them have! We could outrun them, easy!"

At that moment, for some reason, the seals decided they'd had enough of land. The huge male heaved himself up, barked and burped deeply, then set off for the water, undulating his body along like a vast fat caterpillar. It reminded the girls of when they had played a game which involved wriggling along the floor in sleeping bags. The other seals accompanied him - they went surprisingly fast, almost galloping – and in a matter of seconds they were in the water, and their sleek heads disappeared under the waves.

"Whoa," said Rosie, in a more subdued tone. "You were right. We couldn't outrun them!"

"Well, they have my *seal* of approval," punned Rowan, happily.

Rosie grinned. "You're *barking* mad, girl!"

"Arf, arf, arf!" barked Rowan, clapping her hands together like a seal's flippers. Rosie joined in, they laughed so much they almost overbalanced, then calmed down and began to pick their way down towards the end of the rocks again.

"Look, look! It's a *dolphin!*" Rosie squealed with delight.

Rowan didn't say anything, she just stood, drinking it all in, utterly enchanted. The sleek grey shape, leaping up from the waves, scattering water droplets like sparkling diamonds, curving through the air, then down, in a splash of white foam, its rose-thorn fin cutting through the surface of the ocean. Dolphins. She had always loved them ever since seeing them on a wildlife programme once. They were so beautiful, so perfectly adapted to the water, evolution at its best. They liked to play, they were intelligent, sociable. How wonderful to be a dolphin, no school, no tests to pass, no Maxine....

Oh, sugar! She didn't want to think of Maxine now!

How wonderful to be a dolphin, just eating, playing, exploring... But dolphins had their own troubles, caught up and drowned in tuna fishing nets, or swallowing plastic bags and other rubbish humans had thrown away, or getting poisoned by oil slicks, or hurt by passing ships, or trapped in tiny pools and trained to perform for entertainment.

Were there humans in this other world? She hoped they had learned better than the humans in her world.

Rosie was jumping up and down waving, and calling: "Hello! Hello, dolphin! Hello!"

The dolphin stood almost straight in the water, nodding its head back, and let out a stream of clicks and squeals. It seemed to be smiling, eyes bright.

Rosie turned to Rowan, eyes shining. "It said hello!"

"Yeah, I bet it is saying hello," agreed Rowan, going forward to the edge of the rock.

"No, I mean, really, it really said hello!"

"Dolphins can't speak, not like us."

"It did! I heard it," insisted Rosie. "It said hello!"

"Rosie…" began Rowan, shaking her head.

"Listen, I'll show you! Hello, dolphin, hello!"

"Squeal, whistle, click click, chirp hey-lo click!"

Rowan's heart leaped, but she didn't want to be fooled. "Hello," she called. "Hello!"

"Squeal, squeal hey-lo, hello, click, click!"

"Whoa! It really did!" she exclaimed.

"Awesome!" breathed Rosie. "Hello, dolphin! What else can you say? I'm Rosie!"

"Hello Rosie click squeal hello, hello!"

"I'm Rowan," added Rowan, not to be outdone.

"Hello Rowan click squeal hello, hello! I'm Findolf!"

"Findolf?" repeated Rowan.

"Findolf the dolphin!" Rosie laughed and clapped her hands.

"Findolf, Findolf!" The dolphin leapt out of the water, high into the air, twisted, back down into the sea with an enormous splash, soaking both the girls. They both squealed as he resurfaced with a cheeky grin and a chuckle. "Swim! I like swim! You like swim and dive?"

"Wish we could," said Rowan. "But it's too cold for us, we're only human."

"Shame! One day warm, you swim?"

"You bet!" agreed Rosie.

"Yeah!"

"You watch me swim! Show you! I dive and leap good!

See!"

He proceeded to show them the most wonderful acrobatics and they clapped and cheered him on enthusiastically. He brought back some seaweed balanced on his nose, Rowan plucked it off and teased him with it as one teases a cat, with Findolf snapping at it, and her whipping it back at the last minute, and both of them laughing, Findolf remarking: "Funny! Funny!"

"Let me have a go!" cried Rosie, so they took turns to play.

After some time, Rowan looked up and saw the sky turning pink and purple. "It's getting late," she said. "We've got to go."

"Aw," complained Rosie, although her teeth were chattering.

"It's evening here. We can't stay all night. It's probably nearly morning back home."

"Oh, all right, then," agreed Rosie reluctantly.

"You go?" asked Findolf, sounding disappointed.

"Fraid so," said Rowan. "But we'll come back tomorrow, I promise!"

"Good to see you then!" He grinned at her with his curving dolphin smile, and Rowan felt her heart glow with love. "It'll be good to see you too," she said.

"Yeah, bye," added Rosie.

"Bye bye!" Findolf turned and swam swiftly away.

Both girls realised they were wet, cold, and very very tired. It was exhausting to go plodding back through the deep snow and into the wood. The sun had nearly set and there was an icy wind. Rosie began to grumble. Rowan just let her, she felt like grumbling herself, but she knew it had been worth it.

Finally, they tracked their footprints back to the oak tree. They bent down, and crawled back under the hollow, and into the darkness. Back home.

"Ugh, it's started to rain!" Rosie scrunched up her nose.

"Well, we can't get much wetter than we are! Let's get back inside, quick, in case Mum and Dad missed us," said Rowan. She squinted up at the clouds rushing over the half-moon.

Then they hurried back inside, to their nice warm dry house, stripped off their wet clothes, rubbed themselves dry with towels, got into their pyjamas, and fell asleep, utterly exhausted.

Chapter Four

They both woke the next morning ravenously hungry. Rowan blinked, and sat up, rubbing her hair. The light through the windows was dim and grey, a winter morning.

"Rosie…" she began, as the events of last night came flooding back to her, "it was real, wasn't it?"

"Definitely," said Rosie stoutly. "We can't both dream the same dream. It was real all right. There was snow!"

"And a dolphin!"

"Findolf the dolphin!" Rosie grinned.

There was a knock at the door. "Come on, you two, time to get up for school!" It was their Mum.

Rowan and Rosie kept catching each other's eyes at the breakfast table, as they ate their porridge (Rowan's with honey and Rosie's with plum jam) - but Mum and Dad were there too, and they couldn't talk in front of them. Both of them kept yawning. Rowan's head was spinning: she remembered the crunch of the snow, the twinkle in Findolf's eyes, the splash of water as he leaped and landed, the briny smell of the sea…

"What's the matter with you two? Couldn't sleep?" asked Jenny.

"Oh, we're fiiiiine," Rosie began to answer but trailed off in a yawn.

"Your hair needs brushing. Have you got everything? Pencil case? Homework?"

"Uh-huh."

Rowan hardly spoke to anyone at school, she murmured vague greetings to Sarah and Becky, drifted past Maxine and her gang hardly hearing the name-calling, sat through lessons not taking much in at all. *Another world.* And she and Rosie had gone there. Another world and a forest and a beach and a talking dolphin! It was amazing, it was beyond amazing… and today, they would go again today, after school.

Rosie came running up to Rowan in the playground at the end of the day. "Today's been a million years long! Let's go to the tree as soon as we get home," she said excitedly.

"We have to go in and say hello to Mum and Dad first," said Rowan, "else they'll want to know why."

"Okay, and *then* we'll go!"

The bus took longer to arrive than normal, and when they were on board it seemed to crawl, and the distance between the bus stop and home had doubled…

Finally, home, in, had a snack, changed out of their school uniforms, in coats and hats and boots, they were at the tree. The sky was cloudy, the daylight was draining away into greyness, and it was cold.

"Me first," said Rosie. She flung herself flat, wriggled in… and backed out again, shaking her head. "It's not there! It's not there, Rowan," she cried. "Was it only a dream, then?"

"No," said Rowan, her heart in her mouth, her stomach sinking. "No, I'm sure it wasn't, I'm sure!"

"Then why isn't it there any more?"

"Well," said Rowan, thinking hard. "First time you went in the tree, it wasn't there either… I know! We went in at night! I bet that's it, we have to go at night!"

"Bet it is!" agreed Rosie. "Tonight, then! After Mum and Dad are asleep, yeah?"

"Yeah!"

Rowan's stomach was churning with butterflies so much that she found it difficult to eat her lentil cottage pie, even though it was one of her favourites. There were lentils and vegetables in a rich, thick tomato sauce flavoured with basil, pepper and soy sauce, and the mashed potato that covered it had a crispy topping with golden grated cheese and sprinkled with paprika.

Rosie's appetite was undiminished. She ate cheerfully and had second helpings.

"Can't sleep," remarked Rosie, after Dad had finished reading the bedtime story, kissed them both goodnight, switched the light off and left them.

"Me neither," said Rowan, turning over and resting her head on one hand. "Shall we check it wasn't a dream? Exactly what do you remember happening?"

"Well," began Rosie, and they both went through it. Their accounts matched perfectly. They were both yawning by the end, their eyelids heavy.

Rowan woke suddenly from a dream where she had gone back through the oak and to the sea, only to find Maxine and her gang standing there, pointing and laughing and calling her ginger and freak, and Findolf was leaping up and laughing at her too.

"Rowan! Wake up!"

"Huh?" Rowan's heart was pounding and her palms were sweating.

"Wake up! It's time! Come on!" Rosie was hopping up and down with excitement.

"Okay." Rowan pushed back the bedcovers, and swung her legs out. Her bare feet touched the cold floor. They dressed hastily. They both held their breath going downstairs. Every step seemed to creak. They froze - what if Mum or Dad heard? How would they explain?

"We could say we're sleepwalking," whispered Rosie, as

they carefully removed their coats and hats from the pegs by the door and pulled them on.

The cold hit them once they were outside. They could hardly see, the sky was cloudy, the hedge and tree and their garden just dim vague black shapes. Their breath puffed out in steam.

Here was the oak tree, looming and mysterious. A owl hooted nearby.

"Me first this time," said Rowan.

"Okay." Rosie agreed on the fairness of this.

Rowan crouched down, lay down, put her head inside. It was dark, very dark. It smelt of wet wood and earth. There was no light. There was no sparkle. There was nothing. Her stomach sank. She waited, wondering what to do. Would it suddenly happen?

She heard Rosie. "What? It's not there, is it? Rowan? Rowan?"

Rowan sighed deeply, and pulled her head out again. She shook it. "No."

"Oh, *sugar!* Oh..." Rosie clenched her fists. "I want to go back! I want to see Findolf again!"

"Me too. And we promised..." Rowan felt awful. Findolf, someone who seemed genuinely pleased to see them, seemed to like her, and she had promised, and he would be wondering where they were, he would think they were lying, didn't really like him. They had let him down.

There should have been this magical land, and Rowan had felt it light up her life with the promise and potential...but instead... nothing. Just dark and cold, wood and earth.

There was nothing to be done. They crept back to bed. "Maybe another day," murmured Rosie hopefully, but Rowan had this grey sinking feeling. It would be just an oak tree tomorrow, and the day after, and the day after that. Things would go on, just as before.
Rowan cried.

Time passed. There was frost, and sleet, rain, and hail. The horse chestnut tree in the school playground produced fat sticky buds which looked as though they had been rolled out of toffee. Green shoots began to poke their way through the earth. There were snowdrops in their garden.

Rowan kept the secret inside her, closely guarded. Maxine was as bad as ever. She's never been to another world, Rowan told herself. I'd rather be me than her.

But it still hurt. One day she saw a couple of Year Two kids shaking hands and chanting: "Make friends, make friends, never never break friends, if you do, you'll catch the flu, and that will be the end of you!" Then they laughed.

Rowan thought: Why can't I have good friends? What's wrong with me? Nobody wants to be my best friend. Maybe I am just a freak like Maxine says. If I was more interested in fashion and celebrities like she is...

But I don't want to be interested in them! a rebellious part of her would retort. I'm not!

Every word of Maxine's, every look from her and her gang, every spiteful giggle, stung her inside. She didn't tell anyone, didn't tell Mum or Dad. If she did, then it would make it more real. They would be concerned, angry even.

They would tell the school, and the Head would call Maxine into her office, and Maxine would open her blue eyes wide and say: "But I don't know what you're talking about! I'm not a bully! I've talked to Rowan a few times, that's all, just talking…"

And the Head would believe her. And then Maxine would hate Rowan even more for being a grass, and maybe then she would start to steal from her, or hit her or something like that. And Rowan would have a reputation as somebody who went whining to teachers.

The nights passed, the moon became full, then gradually narrowed to crescent, like a sharp sliver of silver in the dark winter sky, which disappeared, reappeared as the new moon, then gradually widened night by night…

"A half moon tonight," remarked their Mum, looking out of the sitting room window before drawing the curtain. It was only five o'clock, and already dark, she shut out the winter night, enclosing them in warm golden snugness.

Suddenly, Rowan remembered. She fizzed all over, leaned over to where Rosie was drawing pictures of guinea pigs, and whispered, "Rosie! Do you remember? It was a half moon the last time we went through!"

Rosie nearly choked with excitement, her eyes bulging.

"Tonight then!"

"Tonight!"

Chapter Five

This time it worked! They stepped out into the golden green sunlight of the other world.

"No snow," observed Rosie, standing up and looking around.

"No. Still a bit chilly, at least the wind is. But there's no frost either. And the sun is warm." Rowan sniffed the air. "Smells good… sort of fresh and…"

"Springy?" offered Rosie.

"Yeah. Like something's going to happen any minute." The trees were still bare, the grass slightly damp, there were patches of bare brown earth in the forest, and here and there were clumps of snowdrops, with their narrow green leaves, and white heads bowed, nodding in the breeze. They could hear the chuckle and swish of the stream. Then there was a rustling sound.

"What was that?" asked Rosie.

"Don't know." Rowan frowned.

"Come on, I think it came from over here." Rosie set off towards the stream, and stopped in front of a willow tree, whose long branches and twigs drooped over the water. The water itself was very clear, they could see pebbles and brown earth at the bottom, and one or two darting little fish.

Rustle, rustle.

"No, it's in the beeches, I think," said Rowan.

They went up the slope under the smooth grey beech trees, their feet rustling through the russet fallen leaves. Every now and again, there'd be a sudden crack as they stepped on the beechnut cases which had dropped from the trees last autumn. Rosie bent down, picked up a case and put it on the tip of her ring finger. It fitted perfectly, and was lined with silvery grey fur inside. She gathered more until each of her fingers was tipped with a little brown hat. She waggled her fingers, making them bow to each other. "Good day to you, Miss Finger! Nice hat! Why thank you, Miss Other Finger!" She giggled. Rowan turned to see and smiled.

Rustle, rustle.

"There it is again!" said Rowan.

Rosie flung the beechnut cases off and scampered after her sister, who had stopped by one tree.

"There's a hole in the tree. D'you think it's hollow inside like our oak?" asked Rosie.

"Could be," said Rowan. "I don't know what would live in there. Maybe a squirrel. They live in hollow trees."

They both approached the tree, and Rosie stood on tiptoe to look inside. "Ohhh!" she breathed, eyes shining. "It's so *sweet!"*

From the hole, a little head popped out, with round ears and quivering whiskers, all covered in the most beautiful silver-grey fur. It sneezed, brushed a strand of dried grass from one ear with a paw, blinked and opened large bright black eyes. It regarded them, and tipped its head on one side.

"I think it's a chinchilla," said Rowan. "No, Rosie, you'll scare it!" For Rosie had reached out a hand to stroke that beautiful fur.

The chinchilla blinked again, ran both paws over its nose and eyes so its whiskers sprang forward, made a couple of tutting noises, then said, "Don't worry worry! Misty not scared! Good day!"

"You can talk!" gasped Rowan.

"You can talk too!" countered Misty.

Rosie and Rowan laughed. "Of course we can talk!" said Rosie.

"But it's surprising to hear an animal talk," explained Rowan.

"Talk, talk, talk! Some say Misty talk too much!" The chinchilla chuckled, and pulled the rest of its round furry body from the hole. "Lots of talking now! Spring is coming!"

"Were you hibernating?" asked Rowan.

"Yes, yes, yes! Snug and warm for winter… have you got a hazelnut about you?" Misty looked hopeful and made little lip-smacking sounds.

"Sorry," said Rowan.

Rosie examined her pockets. “Oh, I’ve got a few raisins! Would you like those?” She held out the brown shrivelled things. To her delight, Misty hopped onto her arm. She was unexpectedly heavy, and Rosie had to hold her arm steady. Misty bent her head, her whiskers tickling Rosie’s palm as she sniffed the raisins. Then, squirrel-like, she picked one up in between two front paws and nibbled at it.

“Tasty, tasty, tasty!” she observed.

“Have the others if you like,” said Rosie generously.

“Thank you, thank you, thank you!”

“I’m Rosie, by the way, and this is my sister Rowan.”

“Rowan and Rosie! You are Rowan-Tree and Rose-bush?”

“No, we’re not bushes or trees, we’re humans,” explained Rowan, laughing.

“Human? Don’t know human… you elves, aren’t you?”

“Elves? There are elves here?” asked Rowan.

“You two arms, two legs, two hands, fur on head but not on body, two eyes, talking - you elves! Wood elves, not sea elves, else you called Seashell or Anen - Anem - Anen-en-en-emone!” reasoned Misty.

“Where are the wood elves?” asked Rowan, giving up trying to explain.

“In trees, of course! But must be spring now, come out! You feel energy, surely? You hear music, else why you come out? Time for spring!”

“In the trees?” asked Rowan.

“We came *through* a tree,” said Rosie. “An oak tree. Like a door.”

Suddenly both girls felt a fizzing sensation move through

their whole bodies, the energy tingling right out to the edges of their auras. A note of music sounded, and a breeze rustled and shook the whole forest. Goose pimples rose on their skin, Rowan's hair stood out - it was the most exciting feeling. She thought of other excitements: Christmas Eve, the morning of her birthday when she knew she'd see Daddy Taylor - but this was something even more exciting. She blinked, the whole of her vision was fizzing too, like it does in the dark, lots of little dots. There was a beat, like a rapid drumbeat, as if to say wake up, wake up!

And then there was a crack! They spun round to see a tree behind them shimmering and sparkling all over with bright green, then the trunk split open, and out stepped a sort of ghost, it seemed, or beautiful spirit - they could see the trunk of the tree through her slender body, with its tunic of green leaves. She lifted her arms up, stretched, and yawned, and as she did so, became solid. At the same time, the bark of the tree healed up, becoming as smooth as before. They could see her bare feet pressing on the earth. Her hair was bright white-gold like the sunshine, her skin golden-brown like the sunlight on the earth, her ears were pointed, her cheekbones high, she opened her almond-shaped eyes and they were bright green - not green like Rowan's dark green eyes, which were a human colour - but the bright green of newly unfurled spring leaves. Clearly, this was one of the wood elves that Misty had mistaken Rowan and Rosie for.

"Linden, Linden, Linden! Good day, good day, good day!" chattered Misty, leaping off Rosie's arm, skipping forward and jumping up onto Linden's shoulder.

"Ohh, Misty, good day!" yawned Linden, blinking. "Happy Spring… phew, I'm still a bit stiff…" She walked over, and they could see she was nearly as tall as Rowan. She looked at them both with interest, and said, "Good day. Who are you?"

"Rowan and Rosie, Rowan and Rosie!" chirped Misty.

"I'm Rowan, she's Rosie," explained Rowan with a smile - Misty was so funny!

"Pleased to meet you," said Linden, looking slightly puzzled. "I haven't seen you before."

"No, we're new here," said Rowan.

"How *did* you come out of that tree?" asked Rosie.

Linden looked surprised. "Same way we all do."

"Was it like a door through to another place?" asked Rosie. "We came through an oak tree."

"No," began Linden, but just then there was another cracking sound, as the smooth grey trunk of a tall beech tree split, and out of it sprang another elf, who had caramel skin, hair a crocus-gold colour, and bright green eyes. He was wearing a tunic like Linden, only hers was made up of heart-shaped green leaves, and his of smaller leaves, which Rowan recognised as beech leaves. Round his waist was a belt woven from strips of silvery-grey bark, and he had a necklace of beechnut cases. Linden's belt was also woven from thin strips of bark, but it was beige colour rather than grey.

"Here's Beechen," introduced Linden.

"Good day," began Beechen, giving a tremendous yawn and stretch. "Good day, you thorough nuisance, and no I don't have any hazelnuts!" he added to Misty, who was bounding up to him hopefully. Everyone laughed.

"I haven't seen you before," said Beechen, just as Linden had.

"They're new," said Linden.

"New?" asked Beechen.

"I'm Rosie, this is my sister Rowan," introduced Rosie.

"Good to meet you... whatever happened to your ears? They're as round as Misty's! And what are you wearing?" asked Beechen.

"Clothes," said Rosie.

"Our ears are meant to be round, we're not elves, we're humans," explained Rowan.

"They didn't know how we came out of trees, Beechen," said Linden, sounding puzzled.

"All us wood elves come out of trees," said Beechen.

"Well, except the flower elves," added Linden. "They come out of the earth."

At that moment, one of the willows by the stream burst open to reveal a willowy elf with greyish skin and long silvery-green hair.

"How come the other trees haven't split?" asked Rowan. "There's willows all along here."

"Oh, there's lots of willow trees, but only one Willow, lots of beeches but only one Beechen, and so on," said Linden. "We stay in the trees in winter, sleeping, and then come out in spring when the land comes alive - everything wakes up and comes alive."

"Because the Spring Goddess wakes up," added Beechen. He breathed in, putting one hand on his expanding ribs.

"Oh, it's good to breathe spring air again, and sense Her energy!"

"Wonderful," agreed Linden.

"So you're sort of guardians of the trees and things," said Rowan.

"That's right," agreed Linden. "You said something about an oak tree?"

"We came through it. Like a door," said Rosie, stroking Misty, who was on her shoulder again.

"Well of course, it would be an oak," Beechen nodded.

"Why would it?" asked Rowan.

"Oaks are doorways," said Linden.

"As their sacred name suggests," added Beechen.

"What sacred name?" asked Rowan.

"Duir. Duir is Oak and also Door."

"It's part of the name of this place," said Linden. "The two holiest trees - Ash and Oak. Nuin Duir."

"Nwin Do-er," repeated Rowan. Bob had once said something about someone being a do-er not a thinker, it was pronounced like that, only shorter, more like dur, but not der. "That's what this place is called?"

"That's right. Where do you come from then, if not here?" asked Linden.

"Earth," began Rowan.

"So you are flower elves!" interrupted Misty. "Come from the earth!"

"No, we're humans. Our planet is called Earth. We live in a part of it called Britain. There aren't any elves there… at least, there are legends, but… well, I've never seen one. We live in houses, not trees, and…"

Linden's face changed from curious to enlightened. "Oh! I remember - our world has a link with yours - there have been humans here before."

"Oh, come on!" said Beechen impatiently. "We'll miss the Dance at this rate!"

Rowan could see Rosie's brown eyes were shining, she was beginning to jiggle Misty around, clutched against her chest, like she sometimes did with Pickle the guinea pig. "I feel like dancing!" she announced. Rowan felt her own feet wanting to tap to a beat that was ringing through the forest, then Linden and Beechen both opened their mouths and began to sing, such a joyful playful song, their voices joining with other voices throughout the forest, and everyone was dancing together, half dance, half game of Chase, round and round and in and out the trees. Elves were springing up everywhere, dressed in green, their skins ranging from the silver-white of Silver Birch to the dark brown of Holly, and all kinds of golden and tan and brown in between, their hair gold or green, black or brown, all of them dressed in tunics of leaves.

Some were thumping the ground with their feet and green shoots erupted from the earth, grew, and then burst into blossom, like speeded up film on the TV, thought Rowan, as she twirled and skipped. This was so different from her dance classes with the teacher counting one, two, three, bend here, point here, and tap and skip and now... This was just dancing the way you felt like dancing.

The gleaming white snowdrops were followed by crocuses,

white, golden and purple. Then came daffodils, not the large ones, but little wild ones, a bright and cheerful yellow. Pale yellow primroses sprang up, nestling in their leaves near the ground, and celandine like yellow stars. Other elves were stroking the branches of the trees and bushes, and they burst forth into blossom, white and pink. Buds swelled on the ends of the trees, but there were no leaves as yet. The air was full of sparkles of light, bright green, yellow, white, like a flock of birds, thought Rowan, only… She stopped dancing, and watched more carefully. The sparkles seemed to form something, someone… someone who was like sunlight, who flung out fine raindrops that caught the sunlight, as though they were confetti, thrown over the trees to bless them.

"Linden," she said to the elf, "does it look to you like a sort of… woman?"

Linden smiled. "Of course, Rowan! It's the Maiden, Goddess of the Spring! Her spirit is here, bringing it to us, making it happen! Isn't it like that where you come from?"

"Not exactly… at least… it's slower. I've never seen a Goddess, but…" Rowan paused. Hadn't she felt something similar in spring? A sort of excitement? Hadn't she smelt the fresh air, and felt wild energy running through her body, as though she could feel herself growing? Hadn't she felt like skipping as the lambs in the farmer's field did? Skipping like Rosie was now, laughing, eyes shining, hand in hand with Beechen, Misty balanced on her head… Skipping like the two hares she could see, dancing round and round each other, bobbing upright on their hind legs… She looked back at the Maiden, who had condensed more into a shimmering figure with long flowing hair; now she seemed to be Rosie's age, clapping her hands and jumping, now Rowan's own age, taller and more slender than before, twirling and skipping, her feet twinkling; now she was a young woman with a woman's hips and legs, but without the stiff awkwardness of self-consciousness of many grown-ups, she was just as playful and joyful and free, leading the procession of elves round and round in circles and spirals, then suddenly darting across the line of dancers so she was in the middle or at the end rather than the beginning. Rowan caught the laughter, and wondered if there was a Maiden Goddess in our world, but we didn't notice her...

But she didn't have time to think about it much, for the cry went up: "To the sea, to the sea!"

"Come on!" Linden grabbed each of their hands, her green eyes sparkling.

"Why the sea?" asked Rowan.

"It's part of the spring dance - we all go down to the sea to watch the birds returning from their winter migration! It's a wonderful sight! Come on!"

So they ran, through the forest, out onto the grassland, up the slope - and there was the sea spread out in front of them. Everyone spread out along the edge of the ridge, shading their eyes from the sunlight with their hands - for the bright yellow sun was shining in their faces, and the salty breeze was ruffling their hair.

Rosie and Rowan squinted, being careful not to look directly at the sun.

"I see them!" sang out one of the elves. "I see the birds!"

"Where?"

"There!"

"Oh, yes!"

"Looks like a cloud of midges," observed Rosie.

"It does a bit, they're so small..." agreed Rowan.

"It's the birds," confirmed Linden.

Gradually, the cloud of black dots drew closer, and now you could see they were not mere dots, but there were wings flapping, now you could hear the cries of some of them. Rowan identified geese, and ducks quacking, and behind them the chirping of smaller birds. It was wonderful to follow an individual bird, to see the way it rose and fell as part of the flock, to lose it in the pattern of so many birds, and to find it again. It was as though the flock itself was a living thing, the edge of it swaying, rising, falling again, as though it was breathing... she realised that the birds made the flock in the same way as the sparks made the Goddess...closer, closer -

Then there was a cheer, and the air was suddenly full of birds, the loud flapping of wings and the cries of birds sweeping overhead. Some landed on the beach, others on the cliffs or the grass, still others flew into the woods, the ducks and geese headed for the river, and there were others with them, huge white long-necked birds –

"Swans!" exclaimed Rowan.

"Yes," agreed Linden. "Sacred birds."

Everybody craned their necks back, then swung round, following the magnificent flock of birds, and Rowan felt her heart lift. Wonderful!

They returned to the forest which was now alive with hundreds of birds twittering, chattering, singing, swooping, darting in and out of the trees, gathering twigs and grasses to make nests, snapping up insects and grubs to eat. There were finches, blackbirds, woodpeckers, wrens, nightingales and wood pigeons, and other birds the girls were unfamiliar with.

Their eyes wandered, taking in the beautiful spring colours. The blossom on apple trees and blackthorn bushes shone pink and white like clouds in the sunshine, the crocuses, primroses and daffodils mingled yellow, white and purple with the bright green of the new grass, the bark of the many trees was greeny-golden-browny-grey, dappled with long shadows from branch and twig. The deer and squirrels were coppery red, and the butterflies drifting like petals were as yellow as daffodils and as blue as the sky.

Slowly the dance came to an end. The elves were making themselves comfortable, some dozing, some talking, some sunning themselves. Rowan and Rosie found that the urge to dance had given way to a warm contentment.

"Come and have a cup of linden-blossom tea," invited Linden.

"Is that okay?" asked Rowan.

"Why would it not be?"

"Well, you're the spirit of linden trees, so isn't it a bit like cannibalism?"

"Not at all! Lindens are my home, so it's natural they provide me with things. They don't mind as long as I never take too much, which of course I never do."

"Anyway," said Rosie, "we nibble our nails and pick our noses!"

"Speak for yourself!" squeaked Rowan indignantly. "I don't pick my nose!"

"Do," said Rosie sweetly with a smug and irritating smirk.

"I don't!"

"Do."

"I *don't!*"

"Please don't quarrel," said Linden. "Have some tea, it's very soothing."

The tea was in carved wooden cups. It was pale tawny golden, with a delicious refreshing taste and sweetened with honey. They made themselves comfortable, Rowan, Rosie, Linden and Beechen, with Misty sitting on Rosie's shoulder.

"Bees love Linden blossom," observed Linden. "They're often round my trees, I'm friends with them. Did you know they're all females, the ones who gather the nectar from flowers?"

"No," said Rosie.

"I did," said Rowan. "They have a Queen too, don't they."

"Yes, and the males are called drones."

"Oh, look it's a money spider!" Rosie smiled and held up her finger, watching the tiny spider as it made its way along to the tip, then paused, front legs waving. "Ha!" Rosie jerked her finger and the spider plummeted with a little silver thread flying out from behind it. Rosie held her hand still, then the spider climbed back up the thread. Rosie jerked her hand again, and the spider flew out on another thread.

Rosie giggled.

"Rosie, stop playing yo-yo with the money spider," said Rowan. "It's mean."

"Only a little bit mean… it's funny," pleaded Rosie. She sighed. "Oh, all right then," and carefully guided the money spider off her hand and onto the bark of the linden tree. The spider crawled around a bit and then started spinning a web between the trunk and a twig.

"I'm rested now," declared Rosie, "Let's go back to the sea and see Findolf!"

"Good idea," agreed Rowan. "I hope he's still there."

"I'm sure he will be," said Linden. "He likes this place, he often visited before the winter."

"Come on then, Misty." Rosie stood up.

"Not me," said Misty.

"Why not? Don't you like the sea?"

"No, no, no, mustn't get my paws wet!" chittered Misty, sitting up and drawing her front paws together under her chin, as though threatened by a tide. "I'll catch cold if I do!"

"What happens when it rains?" asked Rosie curiously.

"I stay snug and warm inside my tree with my seeds and hazel nuts!"

"You know," said Rowan, "I'm sure chinchillas are from South America. I read it somewhere. But the rest of Nuin Duir is like Britain. So how come you're here?"

"Don't know!"

"I do," said Linden, "I remember, years ago, a chinchilla came through a tree from your world into this one. She was pregnant. She went to the Holy Hazel in the Sacred Grove, and ate some of the hazel nuts that were there, because it was autumn. And because they're sacred, she became more intelligent, and could talk our language and understand things. And all her children and their descendents are intelligent too."

"Very bright! Talk lots!" Misty preened herself.

"Well, when you say *intelligent...*" began Beechen with a smile. Which was exactly the sort of thing Dad would say, thought Rowan, as she and the rest of them laughed - that was his kind of humour.

Misty hopped up and down, "But you can't jump as high as me, Beechen! I jump high, high, up, up, up!"

"Yes, that's true," agreed Beechen.

"Watch me!" Misty jumped down from Rosie's shoulder, scampered over to Beechen and then leapt - about five foot into the air - and landed on Beechen's head. "See! See, see!" she said proudly.

"Your paws are tangling my hair," grimaced Beechen.

Everyone laughed again.

Misty went back to her beech tree and started chatting with the squirrels, while Linden and Beechen joined the other wood elves.

Rowan and Rosie went down to the sea. They climbed over the rocks, being careful not to slip on the clinging bladderwrack, and stepped onto the sand. The air smelt strongly of seaweed. There were lots of shells on the beach, those purple and white striped ones with pointed tops, the little pink ones like fingernails, the slate grey mussel shells, and cone-shaped limpet shells.

"Look, look, it's a crab like Sideways!" exclaimed Rosie.

"So it is. Only without the fur," agreed Rowan. The orange-shelled crab was about the size of her hand. It scrabbled sideways, waving its claws at them, trying to look menacing and failing because it was so small compared to them.

Rosie picked up a piece of driftwood and tried to get the crab to grip it with its claws. Rowan gazed out to sea, watching the waves rise and fall, listening to the rumble and crash, wondering where Findolf was. Was he upset with them for breaking their promise? She couldn't bear it if he was. She climbed back up onto the rock to spy out the sea... there was something there, in amongst the rocks. Not a dolphin, smooth heads - the seals again? But no, they were upright and … it can't be, thought Rowan, rubbing her eyes and staring again. Had the glitter of sunlight reflected on the waves dazzled her eyes?

Rosie had no such doubts as she squealed: "Look! Mermaids!"

"They don't look like mermaids in pictures," objected Rowan. "Mermaids in pictures look like beautiful women with long hair, and fish tails. European women, mostly. Because mermaids are from European fairy tales. But the Yoruba people of Nigeria have a sea goddess who looks like a mermaid sometimes. Daddy Taylor told me that."

That had been three years ago, when several girls had been playing Mermaids in a school swimming lesson – Rowan had enjoyed it right up until the point Maxine had looked at her and said she'd never seen a *black* mermaid before… But Daddy Taylor had made Rowan feel a lot better about it afterwards, with his stories of a powerful and beautiful mother of the sea, who was called Yemoja - or Yemana in Cuba, where Yoruba slaves had been taken, and had managed to keep hold of their spiritual beliefs even through the horrors of slavery. Her name meant 'Mother whose children are fish.'

"Well, they don't have hair – but what else could they be?" reasoned Rosie.

Both girls climbed down the rocks, closer to the sea, to get a better look.

These mermaids had tails shaped like dolphins, their skin was smooth, not human even on their faces, silvery white at the front and a deep blue-black on the back. The contrast was clearest on their sleek bald heads. They had sloping shoulders, stocky bodies, and short arms with webbed fingers. Their noses were flattish, with nostrils that closed as slits and opened again as they breathed, their thin-lipped wide mouths curved to smiles, and their eyes were slightly slanted, grey-green, or grey-blue in colour, with eyelashes rather like seals. They were obviously intelligent, rather playful and charming. Some of them had necklaces and bracelets of shells, which clinked as they moved.

One of them was carrying a baby, old enough to sit upright on one hip, a chubby little arm and hand splayed out like a starfish on its mother's shoulder. And then the mother spoke, "Good day!" she said.

"Hiya!" Rosie waved.

"Hello," added Rowan, remembering what Misty had said, "Are you sea elves?"

"We are. I am Seashell," said the mother. "And this is Limpet."

"I cling," explained Limpet shyly in a baby voice.

"Hello!" smiled Rowan, liking them both immediately.

"We're humans," chattered Rosie confidently, "I'm Rosie and she's Rowan, my sister. We're visiting from another world. Have you seen Findolf at all? You know, the dolphin? He's our friend, and we couldn't come back, we were stuck, and..."

"Oh, we can call him for you," said Seashell.

"Like this," began Limpet, he tipped back his head, opened his mouth and let out a sort of cross between a howl and a whoop: "Oh-eeee-ooh!"

Immediately all the other sea elves joined in, a loud chorus of: "Oh-eeee-ooh!" It echoed across the waves. Rosie joined in enthusiastically, but Rowan was suddenly nervous of meeting Findolf again - what would he say?

There was a ridge of white foam like a horse's tail, running along the waves towards them... there was a fin the shape of a rose-thorn... suddenly there was a tremendous fountain of foam and water droplets and a huge sleek grey shape exploded from the water with a triumphant squealing cry, curved through the sky, and landed with a massive splash. They were soaked again.

But they didn't mind, they were laughing, and Findolf was laughing and squealing and clicking: "Hello, Rowan, hello Rosie, good day, good to see you!"

Rowan felt buoyant with relief. It was all right, he wasn't offended! She stammered an apology, trying to explain they hadn't been able to get back, but he just said: "Never mind that - watch me!"

And then they were playing, just as before, and everything was wonderful.

Until, some time later, when everyone was happily tired, Findolf bobbed up to Rowan and almost touched her throat with the tip of his beak. "You have pain, Rowan," he said, turning his head sideways to look at her with one grey eye. "You have secret pain. What is your pain?"

Chapter Six

"It's nothing," lied Rowan, head low, cheeks hot with her secret shame. She could feel everyone's eyes on her, not least Rosie.

"That is not the truth," said Findolf. "Don't you trust me?"

"Yes!" she cried, looking at him. "Of course!"

"Then tell me. I can see it, dark blue in your aura, around your throat. That is pain. Something is hurting you."

"Well… there's this girl at school," began Rowan

reluctantly. "Called Maxine… and she says things to me, horrible things, and I - I - just c-can't…" To her horror, her voice was giving out, tears were stinging her eyes, she was going to cry in front of everybody!

"Sorry to hear that, unkind to upset you," said Findolf and went off into a series of rattling clicks.

Rosie's mouth had fallen open. "You never *said!*"

Rowan shrugged awkwardly. "Didn't want to. Nothing you could do, anyway. Nothing anyone could do. Shouldn't let it get to me. I'm just useless, that's all."

"Not useless," said Findolf. "Good friend."

"Not useless," said Seashell, putting a hand on her arm.

"No way are you useless! She's the useless one, doing that to you!" Rosie's eyes flashed with anger.

"M'sorry," sniffed Rowan, and she pressed her lips together, trying to stop them going the shape they go when you cry.

"It's not true there's nothing to be done," said Seashell. "If we have a problem and we don't know how to solve it, we go to the Goddess. You must go to the Goddess too."

"The-the Goddess?" asked Rowan, wiping her nose on her hand.

"Yes, yes, yes!" Findolf crowed. "Go to the Goddess, and all shall be well!"

"Yes… but not in the sea, not for you. You aren't sea creatures, at least… you are not completely land creatures, either. So, the Holy Ash, which bridges land and sea. To the Sacred Grove, where the forest elves go," said Seashell.

"Come on," Rosie stood up and held out a hand to her

sister. "We'll go back to the forest and tell Linden, and see this Goddess. You know you should always tell someone if you're being bullied! You should've told me at least!"

Rowan put her hand in her sister's, and got to her feet. "I know," she laughed shakily. "It's just… oh, I dunno! I just couldn't!"

"Course you could, silly, I'm your sister! Come on!" said Rosie. They thanked the sea elves and Findolf, and set off for the forest.

"This is the Sacred Grove," said Linden.

"All those trees…" Rowan stared round at them, trees and bushes, standing in a circle. There was a feeling of power here, as though they were aware of her, watching without any eyes. She felt nervous, but also curious.

"Yew, Birch, Rowan, Ash, Beech, Willow, Hawthorn, Oak, Holly, Hazel, Linden, Apple and Ivy," recited Linden. "They follow the wheel of the Year."

"How do you mean?"

"Well, how do you name the months?"

"January, February, March and so on. It was the Romans, I think."

"We name the changing year with the trees. The year begins on the Longest Night with Yew. That tree is to do with death and rebirth, it never loses its leaves."

"Our Longest Night is in December," said Rowan.

"Then there is Silver Birch, its bark white as the snow, next Rowan, and then Ash, one of our two holiest trees. She was the first to come out of the ocean, so our legends say, and she is the one you will see. She takes us into Spring, as does Beech, with his delicate bright green leaves. Then comes Willow, and Hawthorn - it is in blossom in Hawthorn Month, creamy white, and with such a sweet scent!" Linden smiled. "Oak Month includes Midsummer, the Longest Day."

"That's in June for us. Some people go to Stonehenge to celebrate it."

"It is a grand celebration for us, the Mother is at Her peak, the world full of abundance, the Oak is joyful!" Linden spread her arms wide. "Then comes Holly, to remind us that although the peak is over, life itself is evergreen, and then -"

"Hazel! Yum yum, nuts, my favourite!" interrupted Misty, making little lip smacking noises.

"Then my own tree, the Linden, tree of true knowledge, and meeting places, taking us into Autumn, with Apple, abundant with her beautiful fruit."

"Delicious fruit," put in Misty.

"Fruit which upsets your stomach if you eat as much as you did last Apple Month," said Linden with a slight frown. Misty put her paws together, lowered her nose and tried to look both innocent and repentant.

"Then the final month is Ivy," concluded Linden. "So you see how our year turns."

"I don't understand - is the Goddess *in* the tree? How can a tree talk?" asked Rowan.

"You will see," smiled Linden. "She is the Holy Ash, Nuin herself! Come forward with me, into the Grove.

Don't be afraid!"

As soon as Rowan stepped into the Grove, she felt the energy. She followed Linden clockwise around the circle, and as she passed each tree, the energy would change. It reminded her of being in Glastonbury High Street once, walking past different shops. A shop that sold crystals had a chiming energy like beams of light, another shop with woven wicker goddess figures had twining green energy like vines or bindweed, another one with Hindu gods felt different again, rather like warmth and incense. It was difficult to describe what it felt like to sense each energy, rather like trying to describe a totally new taste to somebody who has never tasted it before. Rowan would feel the tingling in her aura and in her body, now soft like feathers or snowflakes, now intense and sharp like sparks, now clear and smooth like ripples of light on the bed of a pool. Maxine's energy felt sharp and jabbing, spiky and horrible in her solar plexus just above the waist…

They stopped in front of the Holy Ash, and Rowan gulped. Her palms were sweating, although the spring breeze was still chilly. The Ash was a large tree, the bark grey-green. The smooth twigs were bare of leaves, only the deep black buds adorned them. The energy, Rowan felt, was rather like the ocean, it seemed to swell and retreat, swell and retreat like the tide on a shore… but when she looked at one upright branch, about as thick as a broomstick, she felt as though it was a staff of power, from earth to heaven, star to stone.

Linden put her hands together, like the namaste greeting of Hindus, thought Rowan. "We greet you and honour you,

O Nuin, Holy Ash," began Linden. She then gave Rowan a significant look.

"We hon- I mean, we greet you and honour you, O Nuin, Holy Ash," repeated Rowan nervously.

"Here is one, a daughter of Mother Earth, who seeks your wisdom and your guidance," said Linden.

The bark of the tree began to ripple, and thousands of tiny sparkles appeared. Moving and mingling, they began to shape themselves into a face, a figure… and an arm and a hand came down and thumped the branch which was now a staff, down onto the ground. Rowan jumped. The eyes of the Holy Ash opened, and saw her, and knew her. There was a nose and a mouth too, it was like a woman, but Rowan couldn't tell her age - was she young, old? Her eyes were green, no, grey, no, green again…

"Welcome, daughter of the Mother Earth," spoke the Ash. Her voice wasn't loud, yet powerful and strong. So not old like an old lady with a frail voice, thought Rowan, but it had such wisdom in it that she couldn't be that young either. "Speak, and tell me what are your troubles."

Rowan's throat had been aching more and more, it felt as though it was swollen with all her unsaid pain, her whole chest was aching with it now. She opened her mouth, wondering when to begin - and it all came tumbling out, the things Maxine had said, the way Rowan felt so helpless and hurt and hated herself for it, all her doubts about Daddy Taylor, and herself, everything.

And the Holy Ash listened. She said nothing, just listened.

By the time she had finished, Rowan felt exhausted, yet

lighter too. There was silence. Rowan waited for the wisdom, the secret, the key… The Holy Ash still did not speak. Rowan felt increasingly desperate.

"You're magic," began Rowan, "Couldn't you give me something - some potion, some spell - to make Maxine stop bullying me? To make her leave me alone!"

There was a pause.

"Please!" begged Rowan.

"You will need to go on a Quest. You will need to fetch three things. Firstly, you will need three Rowan berries from the tree which grows on Crone Mountain. Secondly, you will need a stone from the underwater cave in the ocean that is guarded by the Shark. Thirdly, you will need to pluck an acorn from the Holy Oak, my partner.

"Fetch these three things for me, Rowan, and what you have asked shall come to pass."

Rowan gulped. "I will, but… how am I going to get there? I don't know where these places are. And I can't breathe underwater either."

"Linden will accompany you on the mountain. Findolf and Seashell shall help with the ocean."

"Then I don't have to go alone?" Rowan felt weak with relief for a moment, then nervous again.

"You don't."

"Can I come?" asked Rosie.

"It is not your Quest," Nuin told her.

"Aw!" Rosie looked rebellious.

"Maybe you'd better go home, Rosie, then at least our parents will have one of us back," said Rowan.

"Fear not, you shall arrive not more than an hour after the time that you left, just as long as you return before our moon becomes a waxing half-moon again, that is, one month."

"Okay, thanks." Rowan was relieved.

"But what'll *I* do?" Rosie persisted.

The Ash said, "You may stay here, with Misty, you may explore the forest, paddle in the sea, gather sea shells and pebbles, share food and songs and stories with the elves."

Rosie brightened. "Goody!"

"And, um, what'll I eat?" asked Rowan.

"You will not need to eat as much food as you do in your own world, for this time is not the same as your time. However, you will need some nourishment. Linden and Beechen shall help you with that. Fare well, Rowan, and I shall see you on your return."

Rowan stood straighter, then put her hands together namaste-style, and bowed. "Thank you!" she said, filled with hope and energy again.

Chapter Seven

Linden and Rowan travelled North, through the forest, Rowan's coat pockets well stocked with berry-chew, wrapped in leaves.

"What's berry-chew?" Rosie had asked when Linden suggested it.

"This," Linden had replied, showing them strips of what looked like reddish-brown leather. She had explained that they picked and crushed hawthorn berries, then strained them so the juice poured into a bowl. Then they ground up hazelnuts and added them to the mixture, which formed a jelly, and then set hard when put to dry in the sun. Strips of it were then cut off. It kept for months.

"Let me try some!" clamoured Rosie. Beechen pulled her off a bit, she popped it in her mouth, chewed and her eyes widened. "S'nice!" she reported. "Fruity. Like apples and liquorice, and sort of nutty as well. Why don't we try it with hawthorn berries at home?"

"We're not allowed to eat any berries except blackberries," Rowan reminded her. "Because some berries are poisonous. Better safe than sorry."

As well as the berry-chew, Rowan also had a wooden water bottle. She felt well prepared, and interested in what was to come. They had said goodbye to Rosie, and were well on their way.

They were heading upwards, and the trees they were passing became silver birches with their white bark, neat catkins hanging from the branches like caterpillars, with hazel bushes here and there; and then evergreen pine trees rather than deciduous ones. The earth and dried leaves underfoot became a thick carpet of pine needles. Rowan saw ants trooping along busily, some of them exploring an old pine cone. Then the trees ended, and they turned left, Westwards, climbing the slope of a range of hills, covered with short grass, bracken, purple heather and spiky gorse bushes. Rabbits looked at them curiously with their noses whiffling, then returned to nibbling the grass.

"There she is," Linden pointed ahead.

Rowan gasped. She had to crane her neck to see. The slope they were climbing gradually grew higher and higher until it became part of a mountain that loomed ahead of them, the grasses giving way to bare rock, higher and higher, sprinkled with snow near the peak, which was lost in clouds.

"How are we going to get up to the top? I can't climb mountains!"

"We don't have to go all the way to the top, just as far as the Rowan tree," said Linden comfortingly.

"Phew!" But Rowan still felt doubt, part of her muttering I'm pathetic, weak, no good, I can't do this…

Linden looked at her, head on one side. "Feel your feet on the ground, your roots going deep into the earth. Feel the connection with Her. You have the strength."

Rowan closed her eyes, felt her feet, which were hot with walking inside her socks and trainers. She could feel her heart beating, the breath in her lungs, in and out. Down, down, as though she had roots, her awareness spreading out and down from the soles of her feet, down into the earth… soil, rock… down, down… and it was as though there was a great, slow heart beating, a huge deep humming, an aliveness, and from it, springing upwards, was energy, life, up and up like the way a tree drinks earth through its roots, up and up through the soles of her feet, up her legs, and her spine. She held up her arms, feeling the energy fountaining out through the palms of her hands and the crown of her head. "Whoo-eee!" she whooped, opened her eyes, and Linden was laughing, not a jeering laugh, just an acknowledgement of something wonderful.

Rowan laughed, and blinked. "Thanks!" she said.

Linden smiled, held out a palm to indicate it was no trouble. Rowan looked deep into Linden's bright green eyes, which combined innocence with wisdom. She had seen that wide-eyed drinking-in-everything look in Rosie when she was a baby, she could just remember it. But Linden also looked as though she knew so many things, and had experienced centuries.

"How old are you, Linden?"

Linden laughed. "As old as the trees, as young as the spring!"

"What do you mean?"

"I have existed since the first Linden tree in Nuin Duir, so I am that old. But every winter, when we go into our trees, to sleep, our essence mingles and spreads, like the way leaves rot into the soil, so we are no longer alive in these bodies. Yet gradually, we gather together again, and in the spring, we are reborn into a new body." She patted herself just below the collarbone.

"We live longer than that in the same body. Some humans live to be a hundred," said Rowan. "Our bodies gradually wear out, though. The muscles get weaker and the joints get stiffer and the skin wrinkles, and our hair turns grey. Finally we die, unless we've died before of something else. Then our spirits go to Heaven, and get reborn again as babies when it's the right time."

"So you have not always been called Rowan?"

"No. I don't remember, but I could've been anybody… When you're asleep in winter, what do you dream of? Do you dream?"

"We dream of cosy darkness, of the womb of all things, of the black earth which holds us and nourishes us until such time as we spring forth again. We dream of the Crone, she who is death and transformation, for there is no life without death, and no death without life."

"Lots of humans think death is the end. That's it, you're

dead, you don't exist any more. They're scared of death and dying. Dying can be painful, but I'm not scared of death."

"It sounds to me like they're half right. Your bodies are physical, they break down and become part of the earth again. So you will never live in that particular body at that particular time again. Bodies are precious and should be taken care of and appreciated, not neglected. But the spirit is eternal, ever growing, ever changing."

"Yeah. I'm not scared, but I don't want to die just yet!" said Rowan. "There's a lot to live for. I like being alive." She realised that was true, even with Maxine getting at her. Rowan took the water bottle from her pocket and had a drink of water, offered it to Linden who sipped a little too. Then they set off again.

Rowan enjoyed walking out on the hills. The rabbit-nibbled grass was springy under her feet. The gorse was in bloom, the blossoms her favourite colour of saffron gold like crocuses. The air was fresh, the sky blue with little white clouds chasing each other across it. The breeze ruffled her hair, put roses in her cheeks, and she felt, breathing in, as though her lungs were lighting up inside. A bird was singing, she could see it flying high in the sky, swooping and diving.

"What is that?" she asked, pointing.

Linden looked. "A skylark," she identified. "Two skylarks," she amended, as one was joined by another. They seemed almost to be dancing, chasing each other, then they would circle, turn, and the chaser would become the chased.

As they turned North and made their way up the ever steeper slope, the sun moved through the sky, behind them, then to the left, so their shadows were ahead, then to their right. They had slowed now, and sometimes they would have to go on all fours, finding places for hands and feet. Linden never rushed Rowan, was ever patient and calm. Perhaps being a tree elf did that for you: after all, trees just stood for years.

The light turned golden, and then orange.

"It's time to stop for the night," said Linden.

"All right."

They stopped on a patch of ground with short grass. Rowan sat down to catch her breath. Linden produced a wooden bottle with linden blossom tea in it, and they both drank. Rowan was hungry. She took the berry-chew from her coat pocket and munched it. It was tasty, the slightly sharp fruity flavour making her mouth water, and satisfying as well. She thought of stories she had read: travellers roasting rabbit over the fire, or making stews, but supposed that tree elves wouldn't approve of fire, no more than she would feel comfortable sitting in front of a fire made of human limbs. She wondered how Rosie was, but wasn't worried.

Then she stood up to gaze out over the land. The sun was setting in the West, and the clouds were a mass of gold and salmon pink and deep red, with the black horizon below. Above the clouds, the sky blended from pale yellow to pale blue without ever quite becoming green, and higher up the pale blue grew dimmer, and more purple. There was a single star in the sky. Behind her was the forest, and in front of her the hills, their green fading into blue grey, except where the orange sunlight caught the tops of them. To her right, over the mist-cloaked land, she could see the sea, blending into blue-grey-purple, wrinkles on the surface showing where the waves were. And there was a creamy half-moon, already high in the sky, glowing through the pale misty cloud.

Rowan had thought, as she curled up for the night, with her back against Linden's, that she would never go to sleep in such a strange place. But she was physically exhausted, and swiftly fell into a deep slumber.

She woke to cold, damp dew, sunrise, birds singing, and the ground underneath her astonishingly hard and knobbly. She groaned and opened her eyes. Linden was standing already, looking very refreshed and ready to start the day. "Good morning, Rowan! How are you?"

"Argh. Don't ask." Rowan yawned, rubbed sleep-dust out of her eyes, and stretched her aching limbs. Her mouth was dry.

"Have some linden-blossom tea!"

Rowan felt a lot better after breakfast. There was something very refreshing about the air, as though breathing that coolness and those sparkles was nourishing in itself. She wasn't used to being outdoors for such a long time. She followed Linden quite easily, walking and climbing further up the mountain, until Linden said, "There it is," and pointed.

And there it was, on a flatter part of the mountain, a small grassy patch of land, with a rocky grey cliff face, and in front of the cliff grew the Rowan tree, the trunk about as thick as Rowan's arm, with smooth greeny-grey bark.

They reached the grass and stood in front of the tree.

"But -" Rowan's stomach sank with dread as she stared at the twigs. "But they're bare! There aren't any leaves, let alone berries!"

"Rowan berries arrive in summer," said Linden.

Rowan turned to her, her face twisted with agitation. "How can I bring back berries when there aren't any? Why did I get sent on this Quest if it's impossible?"

Linden remained calm.

"What am I supposed to do?" cried Rowan. "I can't just sit here till summer! It's months away!"

"You could try asking the Rowan Tree," said Linden.

Rowan paused. "Is that possible?"

"Of course." Linden smiled, and held out one hand towards the Rowan. "Go ahead."

Rowan turned to the tree, put out a hand and touched the trunk. She patted the bark. "Rowan tree. Rowan, I'm called Rowan too! Please, I need three berries to help me on a Quest. The Holy Ash sent me. It's because of this girl…" And Rowan explained about Maxine. "So, please can you grow some berries for me? Please?"

The Rowan was silent.

"Please!" begged Rowan. "Please!"

Nothing.

Rowan cried, "Please, you've got to help me, please! Listen to me!"

Absolute silence.

"Don't ignore me! I know you can hear me! Please, help me, please!" Rowan sank to her knees, fear shooting through her, "I'm desperate," she sobbed helplessly, "Please, please! You have to help me! Please, oh -" She cried and cried, then wiped her face and shouted: "It's no good! You're just a tree! It's useless, it'll never work! I'm useless! Useless!" She thumped the ground, she got up and stamped, she howled at the tree which remained just a bare Rowan tree on the side of the mountain.

Then, weighed down like lead with her failure, she turned to Linden, who was sitting quietly on the grass. "It's no good," said Rowan hopelessly, raising her shoulders and letting them drop. "It's no good. I've failed. Can't you do something?"

"You need to ask in the right way," said Linden quietly.

"What? What way? Why didn't you tell me?"

"You were… occupied," replied Linden.

"Hmph." Rowan wiped her nose on her sleeve. "I feel like a right pillock now."

"That is the problem. You feel useless. You are begging, not asking. You are speaking from a space of fear, the space of a victim. In order to receive, one needs to ask. One needs to understand one's own power."

"I thought… I thought it would take pity on me," realised Rowan slowly. "If I showed it how helpless I was."

"But you are not helpless. Your feet are on the earth."

"Oh! Like you showed me before! The connection. You have the strength, you said. And I did."

Linden smiled and nodded.

"So I need to ask from a space of power."

Linden nodded again, green eyes twinkling in her tan-brown face. "And the Holy Name of the Rowan is Luis."

"Luis. Thank you." Rowan closed her eyes, became aware, feet on the earth, heart beating in her chest, breath in her lungs, in and then out, in and then out. Like your roots, Rowan Tree, Luis, she thought, out and down from the soles of my feet, down into the deep earth of the mountain… And there it was, the aliveness, the energy from the mountain, the connection… Like you drinking water up through your roots, Luis, Rowan Tree…

Then Rowan began to sense the tree as a presence in itself, a being with life and awareness, and wisdom. She began to understand the nature of the Rowan Tree, as though it was speaking to her through words and pictures in her mind... like a bright flame, the Rowan protects from all harm. She could see images of people dressed in old-fashioned clothes, putting sprays of Rowan over the doors of their houses for protection, and people in even more old-fashioned clothes planting five Rowan trees around a stone circle. There was a woman in a long dress and cloak with a walking stick made of Rowan, a five pointed star carved upon it, and she was not afraid of the dark for she knew that the power of the Rowan would protect her from all harm…

And it is the way of the Rowan to distinguish good from bad, to protect against that which would trick you or harm you… and Rowan understood that she had been right to think that pretending to be more interested in fashion and celebrities to fit in more, and be more like Maxine, would have been wrong for her. And she understood that she herself was not a freak, that was just Maxine trying to make her feel bad about herself, trying to trick her…

Well, she wouldn't fall for that any more, she would remember the way of the Rowan, like a bright flame of protection to keep the light when there is darkness all around… she could see red flames in her mind's eye, sense the bright burning energy of Luis…

Rowan opened her eyes and gasped, for the twig in front of her was budding, the hairy buds were swelling, and bright green leaves burst out like a butterfly emerging from a chrysalis; the leaves grew and darkened, and then there was a little spray of creamy white five-petalled flowers, which faded, and where each flower had been, tiny green berries were swelling, which grew to be the size of peas, then began to ripen, turning from green to yellow, yellow to orange, orange to ripe beautiful red, red as flames. And each berry had a little pentagram - a five pointed star, on its base. Protection from all harm.

"May I?" whispered Rowan.

And she felt the tree whisper back: *Yess…* and the breeze rustled the branches, the bare ones and the one hung with leaves and bright red berries. So Rowan reached out and plucked three berries, and tucked them into her belt-bag, and then she bowed, hands together, to the tree, and said, "Thank you, Luis, Rowan Tree."

And then another breeze blew, and the leaves curled and dried, and the remaining berries wrinkled and faded, and they fell from the tree and vanished into the soil below.

Rowan turned to Linden with a smile, and Linden smiled back.

They could hear a blackbird singing as they turned to make their way back down the mountain. The first task was done, and it was time to travel to the sea, for the second task in Rowan's quest.

Chapter Eight

"Did you get them?" asked Rosie eagerly. She was waiting by the linden tree with Misty on her shoulder, and Beechen sitting on one of the branches of the tree. He jumped off.

"Yeah." Rowan smiled.

"Goody! I knew you would!" The sisters hugged each other. Then Beechen and Linden hugged each other, and then they all hugged each other. "Did you bring back any hazelnuts?" asked Misty hopefully, smacking her lips.

"No, just rowan berries." Rowan yawned and stretched. She was bone-tired.

"We'll set up a couple of hammocks for you in the trees," said Beechen. "Welcome back."

"Thank you." Rowan smiled, then yawned again, so much that her jaw made a cracking sound.

"Can I come with you to the sea?" asked Rosie, once they were lying in their hammocks. She wasn't that tired yet, she was too excited, and it was fun to make her hammock swing from side to side. Being in a hammock hanging from the branches of a tree in a forest in another world was so very different from being tucked up in bed at home. The air was fresh, scented with earth, wood and spring flowers, and there were breezes and rustlings and creakings from trees, bushes, animals and birds. It was dusk now, the sky above them was grey-blue, and the air was getting chilly.

"All right," agreed Rowan, who was too exhausted to notice much. "In the morning."

Rowan was sitting on a rock, the top of which was dried by the sun. There was a whole heap of rocks, ranging from tiny to enormous, and in between them were rock pools which had wildlife in them, stranded by the retreating tide. There were sea anemones, like marshmallow-sized blobs of jelly, with waving tentacles, and there were limpets, and a crab or two, as well as seaweed. Gulls circled overhead, mewing their plaintive cries. Rosie was absent-mindedly popping the bladders of the bladderwrack weed (which is rather like popping the bubbles of bubblewrap, only smellier!) - and listening to the sea elves and Rowan discussing the best way to go about getting her to the shark's cave for the required stone.

"Too cold?" piped up Limpet in astonishment. "Not too cold!"

"Not for you," explained Rowan. "You live in the sea,

you're used to it. But it's too cold for me to swim for that long. I'd get hypothermia probably."

"We have a layer of fat under our skins which keep us warm," explained Seashell.

"So do we," said Rowan, "but I don't think my fat layer is thick enough! And my clothes will just get wet."

"Hm, so we need something waterproof," said Seashell.

"Skin!" chuckled Limpet, clapping his little webbed hands.

"And the other thing is, it's underwater and I can't hold my breath that long. Less than a minute."

"That's no time!" exclaimed Limpet. "I can hold my breath lots!"

"Why don't you show us, Limpet?" put in an older sea elf, who didn't want any more interruptions because she was thinking up solutions.

"You see, Limpet," explained Seashell, "we are sea creatures and humans are not."

Limpet nodded, mouth pressed together and not breathing.

"You breathe on land, though," pointed out Rosie. "Not like fish."

"True," agreed Seashell. "You know dolphins' ancestors used to be land mammals but went back to the sea and adapted to fit there? Well, we began as elves, and went partly back to the sea, but we liked to live partly on land, like seals, so we evolved as a blend."

"We humans evolved from apes," said Rosie.

"You know, it strikes me that humans may have evolved partly in the sea. You have a layer of fat under your skin, your skin is mostly quite hairless, or has very fine hairs, you have small webs of skin between fingers and toes," said Seashell.

"We have noses, not just big nostril holes like apes do," agreed Rowan. "If a chimp tried to swim, it'd just let water in its nostrils. And apes can't hold their breath, nor can they swim. They just sink."

"I didn't know that!" exclaimed Rosie. "Where did you learn that?"

"Sarah told me," replied Rowan. "She's interested in science and wildlife. We can't hold our breath as long as sea elves, but we can hold them a bit."

"But not long enough to fetch the stone," frowned Seashell.

"No," agreed Rowan, ruefully.

"I know - we can use the charm we use to stop drowning!" said the older sea elf, whose name was Turnstone.

"You can drown?" asked Rowan in surprise.

"We breathe air, we don't have gills. There have been times when a little one has been swimming underwater and got tangled in the weed or something - then we do the charm and put a bubble of air around their head, so they can breathe until we free them," explained Seashell.

"We shall do that with you," decided Turnstone.

"Brilliant!" Rowan smiled.

"And," added Turnstone, "we shall make up the salve we use if we're exploring the icy North."

"Of course! Why did I not think of that?" cried Seashell. "Sometimes we like to swim North to see the magnificent icebergs and the penguins and the white ice-bears. But it's too cold for us to survive there long, so we make a salve of various kinds of seaweed brewed together and mixed with sea-snail slime to form a jelly. Rubbed on our skins, it protects from cold and wet."

"Okay," agreed Rowan. "Thanks."

"Pfff!" Limpet opened his mouth with a gasp. "Held breath!"

They had to travel along the beach, heading South to a place where hot water bubbled up out of the rocks. The sea elves and Findolf swam, of course, but Rowan and Rosie had to walk, and it took most of the morning. But finally they reached there, a rocky shore of pebbles. One of the rocks had a natural cauldron in it, made from the actions of the sea wearing away the softer rock and leaving a hollow.

The sea elves had been there for some time, when Rowan and Rosie arrived, and Turnstone was stirring the cauldron with a stick of driftwood, and chanting.

"Nearly ready," smiled Seashell, so Rowan and Rosie sat on a nearby rock to get their breath back, and dangled their bare feet in a rockpool, as they were hot and tired from walking. The water was quite icy, so Rosie squealed and quickly pulled her feet out again.

"It's ready," said Turnstone.

"Come over here, Rowan," instructed Seashell, beckoning.

Rowan had expected there to be snow, so she had put leggings and a long-sleeved T-shirt and thermal vest on under her jumper and jeans before she had left home. She stripped down to these now, handing her other clothes to

Rosie, and stepped onto the rock, which was cold and rough against the soles of her bare feet. She curled her toes, the soles of her feet felt delicate, and each step towards the sea elves was uncomfortable.

The intensified smell of seaweed, fish and ocean rose from the rock cauldron, as she sat down so that they could reach her - for they couldn't stand upright, but sat, their tails out in front of them.

The sea elves chanted and sang as they rubbed the salve onto Rowan, songs of the deep ocean and the life in it, the clink and rattle of pebbles on the shore, the endless changes.

Rowan helped with the more awkward parts, until she was covered from head to foot - and even the soles of her feet.

"Poo!" said Rosie cheerfully. "You stink!"

"I don't mind," replied Rowan. "I feel warm." She stood up, and the rock was no longer uncomfortable. She walked back to Rosie, and experimentally put one foot in the rock pool. "It's not cold! It's not wet!" she exclaimed.

The sea elves laughed at her astonishment. "That is the point!" said Seashell.

"And we have set the charm for the bubble," added Turnstone.

"Now to try - let us to the sea!" cried Seashell, and the other sea elves gave glad cries of agreement, and squirmed along the rocks in an odd motion, rather like seals, and rather like people pulling themselves along with their arms and hands. A series of splashes, and they were swimming and diving, with Findolf, who had joined them.

"Here goes," said Rowan, standing on the very end of the

rock, looking down at the waves rising and falling and swirling and swishing, her face slightly yellow with nerves and her fists clenched.

"Go on, jump!" encouraged Rosie. "Do it all at once, get it over with! Or I'll push you!" she added mischievously.

"One - two - three!" Rowan closed her eyes, clenched her teeth and jumped, splashing Rosie who squealed and shook her head rapidly like a wet dog.

Rowan surfaced, laughing. "I can do it! I'm not cold or wet! Brilliant! Amazing!" It was strange to feel the waves rising and falling, pulling her up and down with them. It wasn't like a swimming pool, where the water stays in one place, and smells of chlorine. This was a wilder kind of experience.

Suddenly Limpet's blue and white head bobbed up next to her, his cheeks bulging. He blew out water from his mouth in a fountain over Rowan, cried: "Dolphin!" and backed off giggling.

"Dolphin, Findolf, hello Rowan!" announced Findolf in a clatter of clicks and squeals. "Ready to go?"

"I hope I don't fall off," said Rowan nervously.

"Cling like me," said Limpet cheerfully. "I cling and I cling and I cling!" and he tightened his arms and his little starfish hands on Seashell's arm.

Rowan laughed. "Okay, then. I'll cling and cling too!"

Findolf's head sprang from the water, one grey eye gleaming at her. "I'm here!"

"How - how do I climb on you?" asked Rowan.

"Legs wide - I swim under!" Findolf chuckled, and then dived.

"Whoa!" Rowan's eyes widened as she felt him bob up - and then she was sitting on his back, clinging with her legs and her hands on his fin, actually riding a dolphin!

"Ready? Let's go!" cheered Findolf, and they set off, Rowan half turning to wave at the sea elves and Rosie. Rosie jumped up and down, waving both hands madly. "Bye, Rowan! Good luck! Go, girl, go!" Her voice gradually faded as they swam away from the shore.

It was amazing, sitting on Findolf's smooth back, feeling the powerful muscles moving, skimming along the water, the sky azure blue above her, the spring sun shining pale white-gold, catching the tops of the waves and making them sparkle, the waves themselves every shade from azure to deep navy blue, her purple shadow falling to the left of her, the pull of the water against her legs, the taste of salt on her lips, the wind blowing through her hair... such wild joy and such a sense of being at one with everything rose in her, that she spread her arms wide, keeping her balance by gripping with her knees, then opened her mouth and whooped with exhilaration: "Whoo-hooo! I could do this foreveeeer!" The wind took the sound of her cry and stretched it out, flung it far behind her as they powered on, on, ever forward through the ocean.

Several hours later, Rowan was tired, her fingers were stiff from holding onto his dorsal fin, her back, legs and arms were all aching with fatigue. It was nearing twilight and the sky that had been bright blue now had much of the colour drained from it as the sun sank behind them.

"Findolf, where am I going to sleep?" she asked. "I'll fall off if I'm here much longer."

"Of course, you sleep with whole of your brain at once," remarked Findolf. "Our brains only sleep half at a time, we never stop swimming. Don't worry, we nearly at the rocks now, you can get off and sleep there."

"Oh, good." Rowan yawned. Sleeping on a rock didn't sound much fun, but she wasn't going to complain, not when he'd carried her all this way for hours, with only a couple of breaks. She had carried some food with her in her belt bag, and eaten some of it for lunch still sitting on his back, but everything had tasted of salt. Then she had dismounted and trod water while Findolf swam a little way off and then brought his tail down on the surface of the sea with a smack. A couple of stunned fish rose to the surface, and he had gulped them down happily. Rowan had thought at first it was rather gruesome eating fish like that, but then realised it was a lot less cruel than some of the things humans did to kill animals for food, and she ate meat and fish herself. They always bought local meat from the farmer's market though, so they knew the animals had had a decent life, and not been raised on battery farms or been driven hundreds of miles.

"What's that noise?" she asked now. An extraordinary sound was floating over the waves, a shimmering shrieking jabbering echoing multi-faceted sound.

"You see!" chuckled Findolf, and a couple of minutes later, she did. The rocks came into view and they were absolutely covered with birds - white sea-birds, all chattering and screeching at each other. That was the noise. There was a taller stack of rock in the centre of the larger bird-covered rock. On top of the stack was a large nest, with an elegant bird standing there. It was a sea eagle. As they drew closer, Rowan could see that its feathers were brown, with a white tail, and its legs and curved beak were yellow. It looked at them sideways on, spread its wings and ruffled them closed again, like somebody furling an umbrella.

"I ask Sea Eagle's permission first," said Findolf. Rowan herself was wondering where on earth she would fit in amongst all these birds. They were jam-packed together.

"Good day! Greetings!" Findolf reared up so that Rowan nearly slipped off his back and had to cling on tightly to his dorsal fin. "Greetings, Sea Eagle! Findolf the dolphin calls you!"

The sea eagle spread her magnificent wings, which were about two metres long, leapt up and swooped down over them. Rowan gasped at her fierce hooked beak and sharp claws. The eagle fixed them with one golden eye. "Good day, greetings, Findolf the dolphin! And who is this, and what do you want?"

"This is Rowan, a young human who is on a quest with the blessings of the Holy Ash. She needs your help, a place to sleep for the night."

"Please!" added Rowan, smiling hopefully. Whatever would they do if the eagle said no?

"Ahh," mused the sea eagle in her harsh voice, "I have chicks. You won't eat them, will you? Or harm them in any way?"

"Absolutely definitely not," promised Rowan. "It would be very kind of you to help me."

"Very well. You may come up." The sea eagle circled them once more, hovered over her nest, flapped her wings and then landed, and folded them away again.

Findolf swam near the rock, and then dived away from below Rowan, who scrambled onto the rock, her limbs very stiff and sore. She rubbed her arms and stood up on the surface of the rock which was streaked with white bird droppings, and seemed to be rising and falling, because she had been in the ever-moving sea for so long. A thousand birds looked at her and remarked on it noisily. "Excuse me, sorry," said Rowan and started to pick her way through them, with difficulty as their nests were so close together. A vast screeching arose as birds got out of her way, and other birds had to get out of their way, and all of them protested about it. Like the ripples from a pebble dropped in a pond, the chaos spread outwards. It reminded her of being in the cinema and having to squeeze past everybody else to get to the toilets right in the middle of the film, thus blocking their view of the screen.

"Sorry, s'cuse me, sorry…"

"Aak! Careful!"

"Mind my eggs!"

"Don't push!"

"Who you shoving now?"

"Get your wing out my eye!"

"Well, mind my eggs then!"

"Watch what you're doing with your beak!"

"Don't flap your wings in my face!"

"Why, d'you want me to get trodden on?"

"You would insist on building your nest here, wouldn't listen to me…"

"Shut your beak!"

"Aak, aak!"

Flapping wings and shoving, screeching and quarrelling - the din was tremendous, but finally Rowan made it to the stack without treading on a single egg or bird, and climbed up to the nest.

It was made of driftwood and dried seaweed, and inside were two chicks - balls of grey fluff with hooked eagle beaks which immediately gaped open. "Food! Food! Food!" they yelled.

"Oh, shut your beaks, she has no food," scolded the sea eagle. "Sit down, make yourself comfortable."

"Thank you very much," said Rowan, gingerly sitting. The nest was lined with feathers and quite warm, there was a feathery smell rather like the inside of the chicken coop in the garden at home, only mingled with salt, seaweed and fish smells.

"I'll just give the chicks their meal," said the sea eagle, and proceeded to regurgitate a foul-smelling chewed fishiness, poking her beak into the gaping beaks of the chicks, who gulped it down eagerly and clamoured for more. The sea eagle turned to Rowan. "Would you like some food?" she offered politely. There was a thread of fishy drool hanging from her beak.

Rowan's stomach lurched. "No thanks, I'm not hungry,"

she replied hastily.

"Very well," said the sea eagle. One of the chicks gave a satisfied fishy burp.

Rowan was actually quite comfortable in the feather-lined nest with the warm body of the sea eagle covering both the chicks and her, although she did dream that she was in bed at home with the duvet over her face, and when she half woke, she wondered muzzily what she was doing in the chicken coop, or had one of the chickens somehow got into her bedroom? Suddenly, the feathers were gone, and there was air.

"Are you awake?"

Rowan opened her eyes to find the sea eagle regarding her one-eyed.

"Mmff, yeah, thanks." Rowan sat up. "I slept well," she added politely, and the sea eagle looked pleased.

"Food, food, food!" yelled the chicks. The other birds were also waking and beginning to jabber.

"I'll just get their breakfast. Would you like some fish? Whole, perhaps?"

"No thanks, it's all right, I brought some human food with me," said Rowan. "Thank you very much for your hospitality."

"Oh, quite all right, quite all right." The sea eagle preened some feathers on her left wing.

"Is Findolf near?"

"Oh, yes, he's circling round about."

Rowan ate her breakfast as discreetly as she could while

the sea eagle fished and the chicks watched her and clamoured for some. "I don't think nuts and berries would suit you," she told them. Then she had to repeat the same process as yesterday to cross the rock. Only this time, well rested and fed, she found she had the urge to giggle.

"Mind out!"

"Watch it!"

"Don't you push me!"

"Aak! Aak!"

"I'm so sorry, please excuse me, sorry, nearly there…"

When she got to the edge of the rock, she waved to Findolf, who leaped out of the water with a glad cry, and landed with a splash. The sea level was much lower, because the tide had changed, and Rowan climbed carefully down the slippery sides of the rock which were covered with seaweed and barnacles. She looked back to see all the birds ruffling their feathers and shuffling back into place again, and preening themselves.

Soon she was on Findolf's back again. "Sleep well?" he asked.

"Yeah." Rowan smiled. "Let's go!"

They called farewells and thanks to the sea eagle and the other birds, and set off once more.

The sky was grey with clouds this morning, although the horizon was pale turquoise under the clouds. Then it began to rain. The drops tickled her skin, but because of the sea elves' salve, she didn't get wet. "What did you do while I was asleep?" she asked Findolf.

"Swam!" he chuckled. "I love to keep moving, moving all

the time."

"Sounds like my Daddy Taylor, he always keeps moving. That's how he is."

"Dolphin Daddy!"

Rowan laughed.

"I love the ocean," remarked Findolf. "She always changes, yet she always herself, storm or calm, warm or cold, day or night."

"Yeah," agreed Rowan, but she knew she wouldn't want the sea forever. She loved the land too.

"Here is the cave," said Findolf.

"How can you tell? It's just sea," said Rowan, looking around at the grey-blue waves, which were identical to all the other waves around.

"My sound-picture."

"Oh, of course, echo-location. I've heard of that, how dolphins send out these sort of sound waves and they bounce off things, so you can tell they're there."

"Yes. Poor humans, poor elves, can't do it. Must be like blind!"

"Oh, we're all right," said Rowan with a smile. "We're used to being like this… Is the shark there?" she asked.

"Yes. And it knows we are."

Uh-oh, thought Rowan. "How?"

"It can sense electric aura of living beings."

"Oh dear." She had hoped they would be able to sneak in somehow, without it noticing. So much for that. Perhaps, though, if they were quick enough…

"Time to dive," remarked Findolf suddenly and without

further warning, he did. Rowan's head jerked back, her finger clutched tightly at his dorsal fin, automatically she held her breath - and then there was no need, for she was underwater, but there was a clear bubble of air surrounding her head. The sea elves' magic had worked perfectly.

Deep blue grey water was all around her. If she looked up she could see the silvery ever-moving surface, surging up into waves and down again, and little circles of the raindrops as they fell. She could feel the pressure of the tides, and Findolf's powerful body pulling them deeper. Below her were jagged rocks, with long strands of seaweed swaying in the tide…

Her heart began to pound. They were nearing the shark's cave.

As they approached, they could see the shark, a sleek grey shape in the water, circling around a large rock with a dark entrance like a gaping mouth, then darting suddenly towards them. Just as swift as Findolf, thought Rowan, her heart sinking, and her stomach clenching. There's no way we can just dodge it. What are we going to do?

The shark sped past, fixing Rowan with one eye, a grey circle with a black circle inside. It wasn't warm and twinkling like Findolf's grey eyes, it was harsh and cold and merciless. Rowan's fingers gripped Findolf's fin tightly. Could it speak? "Hello! Good day!" she called with a nervous brightness. She let go of Findolf, kicked her legs and swam upwards a little. If there were two of them separately, perhaps one could distract while the other got the stone?

Findolf, though, said nothing.

"Hello, shark!" tried Rowan.

"What are you, some kind of freak seal? Your tail is split in two!" sneered the shark, swimming back again, from Rowan's left to her right, then circling away a little.

"It's not a tail, it's legs," explained Rowan.

"Only two? That stupid! Lobsters and starfish have proper number of legs. Lost some, did you Two-Legs?

"No, I've always had two."

"How stupid! You ugly freak!"

Rowan ignored the scornful tone. "Er, we've come to visit you."

"Ha! Stupid freak and stupid dolphin? Likely story, not!"

"Do you get many visitors?"

"No. Everyone too scared to come near me," boasted the shark.

"That must be very lonely," said Rowan, realising as she spoke that it was true.

"Who, me, lonely? Me? Huh!" scoffed the shark. "Why would I be lonely, Two-Legs? Others are stupid and annoying! I don't want them around!"

But Rowan could tell the shark was lying. She wondered what to say next. Just to accuse it would be tactless.

"Don't want you around either! Get lost before I bite your stupid two legs off and leave you with none!" The shark snapped its jaws together, showing jagged pointed teeth, then darted straight at Rowan.

Rowan backed off hastily, ducking as the smooth grey length of the shark passed overhead, just skimming the bubble of air around her head.

Suddenly Findolf was there, putting his body in between her and the shark. "Grab my fin!" Rowan did, Findolf beat his tail and powered away, away…

"That's right, get lost!" jeered the shark. "Don't want to see you ugly freaks here again!"

Findolf and Rowan surfaced, Rowan thinking deeply. She realised the shark was being tough and nasty to cover up loneliness and self doubt. It must be difficult being a shark. It reminded her of somebody…

Maxine!

It was a revelation: Maxine isn't okay!

She doesn't feel good about herself, thought Rowan. She can't do, sneering and sniping all the time. If she really felt good about herself, she wouldn't *need* to. She puts other people down, makes them feel small to make herself feel big. But if she didn't feel small herself, she wouldn't!

She is like the shark!

But I can't think about that now! What can I do to get the stone?

"Sorry," said Findolf. "Dolphins and sharks old enemies. Sometimes sharks kill dolphins. Sometimes dolphin bunch together, to kill shark when threaten young ones! What we do now?"

Rowan's face cleared. "I've got an idea!" she announced.

After some time, they returned, Findolf darting first to the left and then to the right of a slowly swimming squid, herding it the right way. It had long writhing tentacles, and gave Rowan the creeps. Part of her was a little uneasy. But after all, she reminded herself, I've eaten calamari before, that's squid. And Findolf eats fish, and squid and things... Findolf had told her he always gave thanks to the spirits of the creatures he ate, so they had said a prayer together as soon as they had found the squid. Perhaps on some level, the squid understood what they needed.

The shark noticed them. "Oh, look, the ugly two-legged freak again! Thought I told you to get lost, freak!"

"We've brought you a present," announced Rowan, swimming ahead of Findolf.

"A present? For me?" The shark sounded astonished. "Nobody ever brings me presents!"

"It's this squid. Nice squid," encouraged Rowan, beaming, though the thought of eating those slippery tentacles made her shudder.

"Hah! Juicy squid!" The shark's eyes gleamed, it darted forward, snapped its jaws, there was a swirl of tentacles and black squid-ink - and then the squid was gone. "Made you jump!" grinned the shark. "Could be you, Two-Legs!"

Better a squid than a seal, or a dolphin, or me, Rowan told herself. "Yeah, you made me jump all right," she agreed.

"What you want, anyway?" demanded the shark, suddenly suspicious. "Must want something or you not give me present!"

"Nothing much," replied Rowan in a casual tone. "Just a stone from the floor of your cave, that's all."

"Hah! They worthless! You really freaky to want one of them!" jeered the shark.

"I do, just the same," said Rowan pleasantly, her arms and legs moving to keep her hovering in the water. "Will you promise not to attack me if I swim down and get it?"

"Oh, very well," agreed the shark. "I could snap you up in an instant, I just don't care to right now!"

"I see that," said Rowan, starting to swim forward, "You're very fierce."

"Yes I am, aren't I?" preened the shark. "Go on then, be quick about it!"

Rowan kicked with her legs, and swam down as swiftly as she could, into the cave which was encrusted with seaweed and shells. She reached forward one hand, her skin looking pale and greenish in the underwater light, and made to pick up one of a pile of stones. Suddenly it sprouted legs and moved, proving to be a crab disguised as a stone. She drew her hand back, then picked out one without legs, grasped it firmly, turned, and swam back to the waiting Findolf, who looked anxious. She settled on his back, and called, "Goodbye! I hope your enjoyed your meal!"

"You are very polite," observed the shark. "Goodbye." Then it turned away, and Rowan felt the powerful surge of Findolf's muscles, pulling them up through the water to the surface. They burst out, and she blinked in the sudden light, the bubble popping away.

"Phew!" gasped Rowan, which was echoed by a blast of warm air from Findolf's blowhole. He wasn't entirely sure the shark wouldn't change its mind, so he swam as swiftly as possible, back Westwards towards the land, Rowan clutching the stone tightly, her heart beating with relief and triumph.

Findolf kept swimming even after the sun had set. They swam by moonlight, and Rowan thought it was so beautiful, the inky blue-black sea, and ahead of them a silver path from the reflection of the moon. They followed the silver-topped waves back towards the shore.

It was the middle of the night when they reached there, but the sea elves were there to help her off. She was stumbling up to her neck in the lifting, falling waves, then up to her waist, her knees, her ankles. She was ashore and Linden and Beechen were waiting for her. Rowan felt dizzy with sleepiness, she had only the vaguest memories afterwards of saying goodbye and thanks to Findolf, then a walk in the dark rustling night-time forest with owls hooting, then she was in a hammock which had been hung from two linden trees, and her sister Rosie was a curled-up lump in another hammock nearby, thumb in mouth, eyes closed, deeply asleep. And it wasn't long before Rowan was as asleep as her sister.

Chapter Nine

Rowan was woken by whiskers tickling her cheek. "Good day, good day, good day!" said Misty, making little lip-smacking sounds. "Hungry? Tut-tut-tut!"

"Yeah, thanks…" Rowan stirred. The sound of birdsong echoed through the woods. The air was fresh and chilly, sparkling with new-morning scents. "…and I stink!" realised Rowan. The seaweed-and-fishy smell of the salve filled the air.

"Told you you did," grinned Rosie. She was sitting up in her hammock, pushing away a layer of dried bracken and grasses which had kept her warm through the night. "How was the shark? Was it scary?"

"Very," yawned Rowan, stretching her arms over her head, while Misty jumped off her and scampered along the ground to a nearby tree. "But I got the stone… where's the stone?" she had a moment of sudden panic, then remembered she'd tucked it into her belt bag. "Phew!" She brought it out.

"Can I see?"

"Sure." Rowan sat up, putting her feet on the ground to steady herself. Rosie swung back and forth on the hammock, then jumped out and trotted over, scattering bits of bracken and grass as she went. She held out a hand, and Rowan put the stone in. Rosie turned it over and over in her fingers, a roundish grey stone.

"It's ordinary," she observed, sounding a bit disappointed.

"I know it seems it, but the Holy Ash will know what to do. She'll make a spell with it, something like that," said Rowan.

"Cool." Rosie nodded, and handed the stone back. Rowan tucked the stone into her belt bag, then leaned forward and plucked a bit of bracken out of Rosie's hair. Rosie grinned cheerfully. "They're to keep me warm. You don't need it with that stinky stuff over you."

"True… I'm thirsty."

"How about a cup of linden-blossom tea?" offered Linden, suddenly appearing.

"Wonderful!" smiled Rowan, and blinked sleep-dust from her eyes.

After breakfast, Rowan and Rosie headed for the beach. Rosie had washed in the ice-cold stream, which was very refreshing, but Rowan was still waterproof of course. She wanted to thank the sea elves properly - and get rid of the smelly salve.

The early morning sun shone brightly into their faces, dazzling them, and it was reflected on the surface of the waves.

And there were the sea elves, some swimming, others basking on the rocks, their deep blue-black and pale white skins sparkling with sunlight and water.

"Hey!" Rosie waved an arm and scampered towards them. "Ahoy there!"

Rowan laughed, then joined her sister, running over the tawny sand, with her shadow stretching long and dark blue to her right, then scrambling up onto the rocks, breathing in the clean salty chilly air. It was exhilarating.

"Good day!" called Seashell, and Limpet un-clung one of his arms to wave at them.

"I wanted to thank you all," panted Rowan, reaching them. "For your help."

"That's quite all right," said Seashell.

"It was a pleasure," added Turnstone, and the other sea elves agreed.

"The salve was brilliant, but I need to clean it off now," explained Rowan.

"Of course," said Turnstone. "Rub yourself with sand and soap-herb jelly."

"Er… what's soap-herb jelly?" asked Rowan.

"Jelly made from soap-herb, of course!" crowed Limpet and laughed.

"Here, I'll get you some," said Seashell kindly, and she brought this greenish-whitish jelly-like substance, set into a scallop shell as large as Rosie's hand.

Rowan scooped it out, then mixed it with sand and rubbed it onto her skin, then she washed her hands in sea water. "It feels wet again," she said. "It's working." She couldn't put her leggings and long-sleeved T-shirt back on though, as they were wet, so she contented herself with the jeans and jumper that Rosie had been keeping for her, along with her socks and trainers.

Rosie and Rowan stayed there for over an hour, talking about each other's worlds. Findolf arrived and stayed briefly, but swam away again to meet up with the rest of his pod - other young males. They were going to explore and play and hunt together. Rowan and Rosie didn't mind him going. After all, he was a wild dolphin, not a pet to be kept.

"I have to climb the tree now," said Rowan at last, getting to her feet.

"Cling!" remarked Limpet.

"I will," Rowan smiled.

Rowan was standing at the edge of the Sacred Grove, looking around at the ring of trees. She recited the names in her mind: Yew, Birch, Rowan my own tree, Nuin the Holy Ash, Beech, Willow, Hawthorn, Duir the Holy Oak, Holly, Hazel, Linden and Apple, and the dead tree covered with Ivy.

There was nobody here to help her now, no Rosie, no friend to support her, no Linden, or Findolf, Beechen,

Seashell, Limpet, Turnstone or even Misty. Rowan knew she had to do this alone.

She stepped inside, and it was rather like stepping from outside to inside another place, an impressive place, like a cathedral. The air was tingling with energy. She knew the trees were aware of her. She walked around the circle, pausing to put her hands together and make a little respectful bow at each one.

She reached the Holy Oak. Its bark was rough and grooved, and two large branches grew from the main trunk, like arms. Green moss was on the roots, lichen on some of the bark, which was a kind of greeny-beige colour. No leaves as yet, just the buds of early spring. She could sense his presence, like a huge wise old man.

"I greet you and honour you, Duir, Holy Oak. My name is Rowan," she began, and then she explained to the Oak about her quest. She felt as though he was listening. The more she spoke, the taller the tree seemed, and she wondered how she would ever get up there. But she breathed, and felt her connection with the Earth, her feet on the ground, on the brown fallen leaves of autumn, and below them the soil, and she knew her own strength.

Then Rowan laid a hand on the rough cracked bark of the Holy Oak, and closed her eyes, focusing on the tree, asking permission. Feet on the earth, heart beating in her chest, breath in her lungs, in and then out, in and then out. Like your roots, Duir, Oak tree she thought, out and down from the soles of my feet, down into the deep earth of the forest floor, layers and layers of autumn leaves, fallen and rotted down to make rich dark soil… nutrients in the soil, water in the soil, to be drawn up through your roots, Oak tree…

And, as had happened with the Rowan tree, she began to sense his wisdom, the Oak King, crowned with a wreath of leaves and acorns, solid protection of his Kingdom, father of the forest, Green Man, the epitome of wildness… She saw him as a solid door, Duir, doorway to the mysteries, both protecting them from harm and allowing certain seekers through. Bar the way, or open the way, Duir can do both.

He will open for me if I am worthy, thought Rowan.

More pictures came, oak wood for shipbuilding, for the beams of houses to hold them solid and firm, carved oaken chests, chairs, tables, oak doors… Pigs feeding on acorns, herded by a boy in a tunic. Oak bark set afire, the smoke rising up to cure fish… and long ago, a woman in a long dress with a necklace of acorns to invoke Diana, the hunter goddess… and men in white woollen robes, cutting mistletoe from oak trees with their bronze sickles…

Rowan opened her eyes. The tree looked very solid. He seemed to be saying: *Try, then.*

So she tried. She frowned, examining it for a way up. She reached up, jumping to cling to one of the main branches, and at that split second, suddenly remembered Maxine's jeers of: *Freak!* - like a dagger inside her: I am not worthy.

And she fell, and landed on her feet with only a grazed hand to show she had tried to jump at all.

She breathed. No, I am not a freak. I am not stupid. I am worthy. She reminded herself of how she and Linden had climbed the mountain. She reminded herself of the shark.

Maxine is only scared like the shark was, she told herself. Why should I listen? Guard against tricks and harm, Rowan, Luis…

She jumped again, and clung, like Limpet, and swung her feet and legs up. She was on! Sitting on the branch like she had on Findolf. She crawled along it to the trunk. Here was one branch. Here was another. She squatted, then carefully stood, hand here, foot there, gradually moving, climbing. Cling here, stretch there. Handhold here. Foothold there. I'm doing it. I am climbing this tree. I can do it. I am doing it.

Part way up, she paused, and looked down. She gulped. How small and faraway the ground seemed. Her head was spinning. I didn't know I was this high up!

I can't move!

I can't, I'm only a freak, I'm useless, I'm…

I'm *not!*

Leave all that behind. You've got this far. You are climbing it. You are succeeding.

Rowan breathed, in, out. She placed her palm against the rough bark, leaned in, smelt it. Solid. Real. Safe. Strong.

Yes!

Rowan climbed and the higher she climbed, the further behind she left those feelings of being useless and unworthy.

Finally she was there, high up on the trunk, in between where the branches sprang out of it, like a crows-nest high on the mast of a sailing ship made from oak… The wind ruffled her hair. She could see the tops of the other holy trees, and the other trees of the forest, bare branches in the sunlight. A bird flew past, singing. Sunlight was on her face.

She was so high!

Yet cradled, safe in the arms of the Holy Oak.

She closed her eyes again, to tune in to him. And it was as though two mighty wooden doors opened, and showed her the nature of the Oak… courage, endurance, the ability to overcome and survive, learning through doing, restoring the will and self determination…

Feeling strong and determined, Rowan opened her eyes. There was a twig in front of her eyes, sparkling… buds on the end, bursting… short yellow-green catkins there, then new bright green leaves fluttering like the wings of newly hatched butterflies, growing, darkening… and there were two small green swellings, each in its cup… growing, changing colour… they were tawny colour now, like her skin. She reached forward and plucked an acorn, still neatly inside its cup, on its stalk. She smiled.

"Thank you," she said to the tree. "Thank you, Holy Oak, Duir."

Then she had to climb down again, which in some ways was easier, but in others more disconcerting, as she had to look down, which reminded her how far from the ground she was. But she had the acorn, and that thought gave her strength.

Finally, there she was, both feet on the ground. She turned and saw Rosie with Misty, Linden and Beechen, at the entrance to the Sacred Grove, expectant, hopeful. She felt suddenly weak with relief and deeply exhausted. She had never done so much in such a short time, the walking, mountain climbing, swimming, climbing the tree… Her clothes were covered in green stuff, her hair was a mess and had a couple of twigs in it, her trainers had mud on them, her hands were hot and sore, as were her feet, her arms and legs were aching, she smelt of brine and earth and sweat, she was dying for a nice long hot shower bath at home, scented with the Green Apple bubble bath that Mum had bought, and then her own comfortable bed with the white sheets and the green duvet, and white soft pillows…

She went to the others, and they congratulated her. "Would you like some linden-blossom tea?" offered Linden. "Or would you like to go to the Holy Ash first?"

"I'll go. Get it done," said Rowan.

Linden nodded, understanding in her green eyes.

"Good luck," said Rosie, solemn for once. You couldn't be flippant in a place like the Sacred Grove, although you could be joyful.

So Rowan checked again, yes, they were there, the red rowan berries, rather dry and wrinkled now, the grey stone from the cave of the shark, and the acorn from the Holy Oak.

Then she walked forward, through the circle, until she was faced with the Holy Ash. Grey bark, bare branches, black buds on the end of its twigs. Feminine presence and energy swelling and retreating like the ocean. The Mother of the forest.

Rowan put her hands together. "I greet you and honour you, O Nuin, Holy Ash."

The bark of the tree rippled, with thousands of tiny sparkles, moving, mingling, shaping into the face of a woman, ash staff in her hand, linking earth and sky, star and stone.

"Welcome, back, daughter of the Mother Earth." spoke the Ash with her wise voice.

"Nuin, Holy Ash tree," said Rowan, exhausted, yet full of hope. "I have brought the things you asked for." She opened her belt bag, took them out, and held them in her open palm, the rowan berries, the stone, the acorn.

"Ah." The Ash stretched out a grey hand and took them. She looked at them with her grey-green eyes.

Rowan's heart thumped. She watched expectantly. What would the Ash do next? Chant, produce a cauldron? Make a potion, make her drink it? Or perhaps an ointment, to rub on her skin? Would she curse Maxine? What would she do?

"Well, that's it," said the Holy Ash, and she chucked the things casually over her shoulder. They flew through the air, fell, and were completely lost in the undergrowth.

Chapter Ten

"NO!" Rowan shrieked. She ran to find them, scrabbling among nettles and brambles that stung and tore her hands.

"Leave them," instructed the Ash.

"But," Rowan stood, tears pouring down her cheeks as she sobbed desperately, "I *got* them, I got them like you said and it was so much trouble and now you just chuck them away like it was nothing! Like they're worthless! Why? *Why?!"*

"The objects themselves are worth very little," replied the Ash.

"Well why did you send me all the way to the top of the mountain and the bottom of the ocean to *get* them then?"

yelled Rowan, leaving the undergrowth to face the Ash, and stamping her foot in fury and frustration.

"Why do you think?"

Oh, the Ash was being so infuriatingly calm! "I don't *know!* How should I know? *You're* the magic one, or so I thought! You're supposed to be wise and all that, and you send me on this quest, and then I come back and it's all been for nothing!"

"Nothing? Is that what you really feel? Have you learned nothing then?"

"I -" began Rowan, and then paused, thinking. What had she learned?

She had learned that there was no particular reason why people couldn't be friends with her. Linden was her friend, Findolf, Seashell and Limpet. True friends, they had worked as a team.

From climbing in the mountain and getting to know the Rowan tree, she had learned that you need to ask in the right way, and also to connect with the Earth in order to stay strong, and that she herself wasn't helpless and weak. Just breathe, and connect, and you are strong. And also she had learned some of her own nature as Rowan, guarding against tricks and those who would do her harm. Harmful ideas, like pretending to be what you're not just to fit in.

She had learned, from the shark, that people are often fierce and snappy to cover up their own fears, and that unpleasant people are lonely and scared inside, and that sometimes by being nice and polite to them you can make it better.

She had learned that she did have courage, the courage to do things alone, like climbing the oak tree. And she had endured, she had survived the Quest.

It was Daddy Taylor who had told her: *Nobody makes you feel inferior without your consent.* She realised that she had been doing Maxine's job for her, putting herself down, calling herself pathetic and useless and wrong. She would stop that now.

"Oh," she said. "Yes, I learned some things, but…"

"The power is not in the objects. The power is within you."

Learning through doing, thought Rowan, that was part of the way of the Oak… And she sensed the way of the Ash, the tree of rebirth, the keys to the future. Of how your actions affect things, like the way other people treat you, of how that knowledge meant she *could* change, and if she changed, then the situation would change.

"You mean… I *have* changed."

"We all have the power to change," said Nuin the Holy Ash, and then Rowan truly understood, and knew she would carry it all with her when she went back to her own world.

CHAPTER ELEVEN

"Oh, look, it's the ginger freak. How are you doing, ginger? When are you going to get a coat that doesn't clash with your hair?"

"When are you going to buy something that's not from a jumble sale?" Snicker, snicker.

Rowan turned round to see Maxine's sneering face, and the faces of her gang grinning maliciously. But as she remembered Nuin Duir, she breathed and felt her feet rooted on the ground, strong like a tree and she felt her own power strong inside her. She remembered the snappy shark. She wasn't afraid any more. She smiled calmly. "I'm sorry, Maxine."

Maxine blinked. "Sorry?"

"I'm sorry you feel so bad about yourself that you want to put other people down."

"What? What're you on about? That's rubbish," blustered Maxine, but Rowan could see the fear in her eyes. The others in her gang were looking startled and uncertain.

Rowan turned and began to walk away, walking on air, thinking: Yes! I did it! I faced her, and spoke, and wasn't helpless, and I told the truth! She *did* feel genuinely sorry for Maxine. To be unhappy with yourself, snappy and lonely like the shark, afraid inside… horrible.

Maxine shouted furiously after her. "That's rubbish, Rowan Meadows! You ginger! You're just a stupid freak! *Freak!*"

"Maxine!" It was the shocked voice of a teacher. Rowan slowed down a little.

"I'm surprised at you, speaking to someone like that! It's totally unacceptable!"

"Oh, um, er, it was just a joke, Miss, nothing serious…"

"Joke?! That sort of language is not a joke. I am very disturbed to hear you calling names like that. I want you to apologise to Rowan right now. Rowan! Come here!"

Rowan turned, floated dreamily back. When Maxine, her face flaming red, mumbled a reluctant "Sorry," Rowan said heartily: "Apology accepted!" and beamed.

The teacher looked pleased. "That was very graceful of you, Rowan. Well done."

Rowan smiled and went to find Sarah and Becky. Maxine had totally lost her power over her. Things would never be the same again.

Sarah and Becky were both laughing.

"It was so funny, we were out shopping and there was this woman staring at Sarah," gasped Becky, "and so she did her speaker, and said –"

"There is no need to stare. I know I am cool," supplied Sarah.

"And her face was like:" Becky put on a goggle-eyed jaw-dropped look. "And she was like: 'Oh, I'm sorry, I, er, er,' walk off quick, beetroot face!"

Rowan laughed.

"What is the Latin name of the bottlenose dolphin?" asked Sarah.

"I don't know, but I like dolphins," said Rowan.

"Oh, me too," Becky's eyes lit up. "I love them, it's so amazing the way their sonar works, it's like bats, you know…"

"Tursiops truncatus. They are perfectly designed to swim," put in Sarah.

They talked enthusiastically about dolphins, then Rowan took a deep breath, remembering about asking in the right way, and said, "Um. It's my birthday soon, and I was wondering… would you both like to come round for tea?"

They looked pleased, she was glad to see.

"Yes, I would," replied Sarah.

"Me too," said Becky. "We were just saying this morning how you never invite us round, and we wondered why, and Sarah said maybe you were shy or maybe you had a big secret like you turned into a werewolf in the evenings…"

"Or your Dad is a mad scientist who does experiments." Sarah's eyes gleamed. "And there is a monster in the cellar."

"No monster, just my little sister," laughed Rowan. "Well, no, that's mean, she's not a monster really. We've got a couple of guinea pigs."

"Oh, they're cute! I'd love to have a guinea pig!" exclaimed Becky.

"Does your Dad do experiments on them?" asked Sarah.

"No," said Rowan. "Dad cooks, though. He's good at cake. And my Daddy Taylor sings."

"Sometimes I would like it if they made a machine to sing," observed Sarah.

Rowan lay in bed, basking in the fact that she would see Daddy Taylor today, and for a whole week. She was remembering things about him. One time she had grumbled: "Taylor is such an ordinary name! It's boring!" To which Daddy had responded: "Tailors sew pieces of cloth together to make clothes. I sew words together to make poems and songs!"

She'd liked that.

And she would be eleven years old.

And she knew Dad had baked a cake, a lemon one, because she loved lemon flavour. Lemon sponge studded with lemon peel, and lemon curd in between the two layers, and lemon-buttercream on top, with crystallised lemon pieces to decorate it. And there would be presents, she didn't know what but she had some lovely ideas. Rosie had been very secretive. She kept looking at Rowan with her brown eyes sparkling with forbidden knowledge, and Rowan knew Rosie had drawn her a big card. She had deliberately not looked under the pile of Rosie's comics, although she'd seen the edge of it sticking out. There would be tea, Mum had stocked the larder with all sorts of goodies. Sarah and Becky would be there to share it all, the start of a new phase of their friendship. And Daddy Taylor who would sing for them, and with them, and he'd probably tell stories too. She would be so proud to introduce him to them, and them to him.

She could hear birds singing outside. I know how you feel, she thought, hugging herself gleefully.

Daddy Taylor's skin was brown, and his black hair was in jaw-length dreadlocks that were the width of Rowan's little finger. He had a small, neat beard, an infectious smile, and his dark brown eyes seemed almost to glow with all that he carried, the stories, the songs, the sagas of his soul. Today he was wearing a baggy white shirt with a waistcoat made of patchwork, purple, blue, and black, his jeans were blue, and his boots were black. A thin gold chain gleamed against the skin of his neck.

He walked so gracefully, Rowan had thought when he first arrived, as though he was dancing. Then his grin had beamed across to her like a wonderful electric shock, and she had flung herself at him. He caught her in his arms and she lost herself in the joy of the moment.

But the greetings were all over, and he was in the sitting room with her now, tuning his acoustic guitar, then placing it on a chair and bringing his African drum from a box, brushing it down as though it was a horse, or some other pet, and Rowan was gazing at him and thinking again. Taylor Rivers never stayed long in one place. Rowan could see how he would hate to be tied down, he was like Findolf the dolphin, she thought, he loved to be always moving. The whole Earth was his home. That was why it would be cruel to expect him to stay here, in one place, just as it would be cruel to keep Findolf in a cage. Knowing that, she didn't mind that he didn't live here with her. That was his nature, and she loved him just as he was.

"I've composed a new song for you, Rowan," he said with a smile. "Would you like to hear it?"

"Yes, please!" said Rowan, her golden-brown cheeks pinking with pleasure.

She watched his hands tapping on the drum, clever brown fingers with the nails as pink as seashells, bringing up the beat that made her own body sway.

And then he began to sing:

"Ride the dolphin! Oh, ride the dolphin, my daughter,
Cross the waves of the silvery sea,
Ride in sunlight, ride in moonlight,
Grace and beauty, powerful and free!"

Rowan's jaw dropped open as she let out a little whimper of amazement.

He paused. "What's the matter?"

"How did you kno- ?" she paused. "I mean, why a dolphin?"

"I had a dream, a dream of you, my daughter, riding a dolphin through a silver sea." He smiled, lifted one hand to gesture, his fingers rippling like waves. "It was such a powerful beautiful dream, I knew I had to write it! One day maybe I'll take you somewhere to meet a real dolphin. Ireland, perhaps."

"Oh, yes please! Thanks! It's a wonderful song, it makes me tingle all over!"

Daddy Taylor looked at his daughter, her green eyes shining, like her mother and yet not like. Rowan's mother Jenny, who had understood his need to roam, who had wept but let him go - how he had blessed her for that! How glad he had been when she had met Bob Meadows, a man who would love her and help make her a home like she wanted, like she needed. For Jenny was like a tree, who needs a home to blossom and thrive, but he, Taylor, was like a dolphin or a swift, he always needed to be moving. That was his nature. And his daughter, Rowan, would she be a home-loving girl, or a traveller? He didn't yet know, sometimes he thought one thing, sometimes another. But he knew that whatever she was, she was herself, unique, and he loved her for that more than anything.

She was reaching out to him now.

Daddy Taylor hugged her, his big warm comforting arms around her. His dark brown eyes were glowing. "That's my girl," he said.

Rowan's heart was as warm as melted chocolate with love for her Daddy. She was proud to be his girl, and she knew, one hundred percent, that he loved her.

And she was proud to be herself too, Rowan Rivers Meadows. *Glad* to be herself in a way that Maxine simply wasn't.

And the next half-moon… it would be back through the doorway in the oak tree, to see her friends again!

Quirky Dragon - Beyond The Ordinary

Books by Philippa Drakeford

Coming soon:

Danger Through The Oak.

Rowan and Rosie don't much like their cousin Holly. She is rude, fashion-obsessed and thinks them silly and babyish. So when Holly comes to stay, they are glad to escape through the hollow oak to the land of Nuin Duir. Unfortunately, Holly finds her way in too, and worse still, falls into the hands of the sinister inhabitants of the Mall, which is threatening the very future of Nuin Duir.

Available now:

Jasmine & Jade: Totally Friends

"Please, Goddess, send me a friend
who knows about the same things I know."
"Please God, send me a friend!
Send me a girl about my age who believes in angels too!"
Jasmine and Jade become best friends as soon as they meet. It's absolutely, totally wonderful, because they both know their guardian angels! Jasmine can see angels.
Jade can't, but she can sense them, like tingly music nearby.
There's so much to explore.
Jasmine's Mum and Jade's Dad are getting on really well too - but then there's a horrible misunderstanding, and they quarrel. Can Jasmine and Jade's friendship survive?

quirkydragon@yahoo.co.uk

About The Author

Philippa Drakeford has been creating stories since she was a child, fuelled by an avid appetite for reading a varied collection of books, which was encouraged by her understanding parents and aided by excellent public libraries. This love of reading has in no way diminished as an adult.

"I am inspired to write about things that are beyond the ordinary, touching on the magical and spiritual," says Philippa. "I was brought up as a Quaker, and have had an interest in different spiritual traditions for a long time. My stories tend to explore themes that fascinate me, such as the effect of cultural expectations on people. I love to 'get inside the head' of people from different times and different cultures. I enjoy overturning stereotypes. I love humour and have been known to produce some excruciating puns. Nature is very important to me."

Philippa is an illustrator by trade and has worked for prestigious titles, publishing houses and individuals. Commissions include *No Other Blue*, poetry by acclaimed poet and comedian Craig Charles (Red Dwarf, Coronation Street); and award-winning *Inclusion In The Primary Classroom* by Margaret Collins.

Published by Appleseed Press, a small collective of authors.

www.appleseed-press.co.uk
quirkydragon@yahoo.co.uk